W9-AVM-021

A JOB FOR
HANNAH AND
THE HORSEMAN

A JOB FOR HANNAH AND THE HORSEMAN

•

Johnny D. Boggs

AVALON BOOKS
NEW YORK

PRINTED IN THE UNITED STATES OF AMERICA
ON ACID-FREE PAPER
BY HADDON CRAFTSMEN, BLOOMSBURG, PENNSYLVANIA

For all of my cousins:
Those who picked on me, and those I picked on;
Those too old for me to remember;
And those too young to remember me.

Chapter One

"Goober, mister?"

The kid came into focus slowly, a bright-eyed boy with a runny nose dressed in a one-piece blue suit and matching Tam O'Shanter hat with red ribbon. His outstretched right hand held a soggy paper sack of boiled peanuts, while his left hand reached into the bag, withdrew a small goober pea, and stuck it in his mouth, soft shell and all. The boy, still holding the bag, chewed and swallowed . . . everything.

Pete Belissari tasted warm, salty blood as he stared at the lad, a stranger to him. The suit the kid wore came with a skirt. Dressed like a girl. Pete wondered if his parents had dressed him that way when he was that age, five maybe, no older than six. He reached up with his right hand and wiped the blood seeping from his nose and through his mustache. Behind him, the

1

crowd cheered another contestant trying to ride a Brahma bull.

The kid still held the bag of peanuts.

"No thanks, son," Belissari said. He had never been a fan of goobers anyway, and right now he didn't feel like chewing anything. His teeth had slammed together during his three-second ride on the back of Bad Temper, a black bull that lived up to his moniker. Pete tested his jaw as the boy disappeared, peanuts and all, behind the loading chute.

Slowly, Belissari pulled himself out of the dirt and peered beneath the fence just in time to see another bull send its rider skyward like a rag doll. The black cowboy, one of rancher Julian Cale's hired hands, landed in a cloud of dust and quickly rolled underneath the fence to escape the bull's horns and hooves as the spectators gasped, then applauded.

"You tell me," a voice behind Pete began, "what ridin' an ugly bull like that has to do with cowboyin'?"

Belissari rubbed his sore neck as he turned to face one-eyed Buddy Pecos, dressed in shotgun chaps, stovepipe boots, and a black Boss of the Plains Stetson. The left side of his cheek bulged as if he were cursed with some awful deformity, highlighting the old Confederate war horse's facial scars and powder burns. Pecos tried to drown a scurrying centipede with brown tobacco juice, then shifted the massive chaw to the other side of his mouth.

"I don't think bullriding has a thing to do with being a cowboy," Pete answered, testing his nose again, satisfied that the bleeding had stopped. "Just a new contest to give us something to do, something to bet on."

The Texan grinned. "Hope you didn't bet on yourself, pard."

"Not hardly."

Pete Belissari, thirty-one years old, had never considered himself a cowboy, although he had cowboyed lately. A fair-to-middling hand with a lariat, he knew better than to bet on himself in steer roping or something a good cowhand did to earn his thirty dollars a month and found. Riding broncs, though, well, Pete had plenty of experience in those kind of events. He had been a mustanger for several years, providing remounts for the U.S. Army at Fort Davis and West Texas ranches before the market dried up. But riding bulls? That was anyone's game.

Pecos took a place against the corral. "Who was that boy you was talkin' to?"

"Never saw him before."

Belissari turned to watch the next rider. They had come to the Pecos City Rodeo, a Fourth of July celebration the local ranchers and cowboys had started four or so years earlier that kept growing each year. At first, it had been an excuse to see which ranch had the best riders and ropers. They'd lasso and throw steers, ride bucking broncs, run a couple of horse races, pitch horseshoes, throw washers, spit tobacco juice, and shoot targets with revolvers, rifles, and shotguns. The ladies brought cobblers, fried chicken, mashed potatoes, lemon cookies, cured hams, other dishes, and plenty of tea and coffee. The children had a hotcake eating contest, sack races, and recitations of the Declaration of Independence. The good Rev. Cox from Fort Davis's Presbyterian Church held a bible study, and inside the army tent behind the loading chutes, former Sgt. Major Cadwallader sold home-brewed whiskey. This year, Julian Cale had brought three bulls to the rodeo to introduce a new contest for willing participants. Bullriding. The crowd seemed to like the event, if the bulls didn't. Of course, the bulls seemed to be winning. If this had been a baseball game, Pete would have tallied the score as Bulls 13, Cowboys 0.

Nope, 14–0, as another cowhand crashed into the dust.

"Seems like we ought to do somethin' 'bout them rules," Pecos said. "Ain't a body 'round these parts who can ride a bull to a standstill."

Belissari nodded. "Maybe say whoever stays on the longest wins."

A man in a plaid sack suit stepped onto a platform and brought a red, white, and blue megaphone to his mouth. "Ladies and gentlemen," he said, "as soon as our cowboys get Davy Crockett back inside his pen, we'll have our last bullrider of the day, Cowboy Christopher of Fort Davis's Wild Rose Ranch."

Buddy Pecos almost swallowed his tobacco, and Pete Belissari mumbled, "Uh-oh." The Wild Rose was Hannah Scott's spread, which meant Cowboy Christopher had to be young Chris, a teenage orphan. Chris hadn't told anyone he planned on riding one of Julian Cale's Double Rail C bulls, and Hannah would raise holy. . . . Pete saw her then, a tan, blond-haired woman in pink dress and straw hat making her way down the aisle, circling the corral, heading toward the chute. She'd give Chris an earful, then jerk him into the stands. And, if Buddy and Pete were nearby, she'd probably tear their heads off, blaming them for trying to get one of her "children" maimed for life.

Which is why Pete grabbed a lariat, mounted his gray mustang, Poseidon, and rode into the corral. Hey, the two cowboys trying to lead the brindle bull Davy Crockett back into his chute weren't having much luck. It was his duty to help the boys—anything to get out of Hannah's path. The love of Pete's life, but not a woman to trifle with or be within striking distance of when she was hot.

Which is why Buddy pulled his hat down low, mounted his blue roan gelding and followed Pete, thanking the Mexican *vaquero* who closed the gate behind him.

Pecos shook out a loop and let his lariat sail over the snorting Davy Crockett's horns. The hemp ropes of Pecos and two cowboys stretched. The bull snorted, digging his powerful feet into the soft Pecos sand. Belissari swung around the bull, and popped the muscular animal's rear end with the knotted end of his rope. One cowboy's lariat popped, the noose staying on the bull's horns while the long end sang out and shot back, almost poking the waddie's eye out. His horse whinnied and reared, but the cowhand kept his seat.

The crowd applauded.

Hands on her hips, Hannah Scott walked on.

Pete popped the bull again, then rode forward and dropped his loop over Davy Crockett's horns. Well, almost. The bull snorted, shaking his head, and the end of the reata fell to the dust.

The crowd booed and laughed.

Hannah Scott continued to make a beeline for the bull chutes.

And Pete, shaking his head, gathered up his rope and tried again. This time the loop took hold, and Belissari kicked the mustang into a trot and rode ahead, pulling the lariat tight, feeling Poseidon strain under him as they pulled the bull toward the pen. Eventually, they got Davy Crockett inside, shook loose their lariats, and galloped out of the pen before another cowhand closed the gate just as the bull rammed the cedar rails.

As the crowd cheered, Pete, Buddy, and the other cowboy gathered up their ropes.

Helping with the bull had been a tactical error, Pete realized as he secured the lariat on his saddle horn and noticed he was parked in front of the chute containing one Double Rail C bull, Cowboy Christopher, and, now, Hannah Scott.

"Get off that bull right this instant, young man," she told him.

"No, Mama Hannah. This is something I gotta do."

"Christopher!"

"No, Mama Hannah. I already paid my two-bits entry fee."

Her face shot up, and those blue eyes glared as she took in Pete. "Pete," she demanded, "make him stop this tomfoolery."

Belissari looked around for help, but the cowardly Buddy Pecos had ridden to the other side of the corral with the two other cowboys. Pete eyed Chris, shook his head and said, "Chris, that's Bad Temper you're on. You saw what he did to me."

"Yes sir."

The bull lurched in the pen. Poseidon shied away from the snorting bull, and Hannah slipped off the pen rails. The man with the megaphone picked that moment to cry out, "Let'r rip," and the two cowboys beside the chute opened the gate, and Bad Temper, with young Chris holding onto a rope with both hands, bolted across the corral, kicking up dust.

"Chris!" Hannah began, but her shout was lost in the roar of the crowd.

Pete twisted in the saddle, holding his breath. Chris's legs went one way, and his body shot back and forward, almost ramming his face into the bull's head. Still the boy held on, although he moved so fast and in so many directions, Pete ached for him. Belissari turned Poseidon around to face the action. By now the bull had traveled halfway across the arena, its hind legs kicking high, arching its back, snorting, churning up thick Pecos dust.

The orphan's gray hat sailed into the stands. Still, he held tightly. Pete realized he was counting off seconds.

Six . . . seven . . . eight . . .

Chris's left hand shot skyward, above his head, waving frantically. The crowd cheered wildly. The military band, which had come up all the way from Fort Davis, broke into *Yankee Doodle Dandy*. The bull spun around, swinging its hind end like . . . well, Pete had never seen anything like it.

"Man," one of the nearest cowhands said, "that there's one rank bull."

Eleven . . . twelve . . . thirteen . . .

Unbelievable. Chris had stayed on ten seconds longer than Pete had, seven seconds longer than anyone else . . . and still he rode.

Sixteen . . . seventeen . . . eighteen . . . nine—

There! Chris shot up like a cannonball. The bull spun around and charged toward Pecos, who spurred his gelding out of the way. Chris landed on his feet, fell, sprang up and leaped onto the fence, hugging the post and scrambling to the top, pumping his right hand in victory as hundreds of witnesses cut loose with Yankee hurrahs, Rebel yells, shrill whistles, and even a stream of blasphemy.

The band went straight into *Camptown Races*.

Smiling, Pete looked back at Hannah. "Well, Mama Hannah, what do you say about that?"

She started to grin, then brought both hands to her mouth, eyes wide, face losing all color.

Belissari shot around, couldn't believe it. There came the boy, the kid in the girly clothes who had offered Pete the goober peas, walking through the center of the corral, still holding the soggy bag, heading toward triumphant Christopher. The crowd's cheers transformed into short breaths, prayers and, finally, frightened silence. The band stopped playing. Chris turned around, mouth open, eyes wide.

And Bad Temper, snorting, shook its head, slinging snot across the arena, began digging a ditch with its front hooves, and charged the little boy.

Poseidon took off at a gallop even before Belissari

could kick the mustang's sides hard with his Apache-style moccasins. Pete headed straight for the bull, like a bullet, jaw set, leaning forward in the saddle. He saw the boy turn and stop, still holding the bag as if offering Bad Temper some goobers. Pete held his breath, said a quick *táma*, and kicked free of the stirrups just before Poseidon broadsided the charging bull. Many years ago, back in Kentucky while attending the University of Louisville, Belissari had seen a locomotive run over a buckboard that had been crossing the tracks on the edge of town. The train had dragged the wreckage under its cowcatcher until it squealed and screamed to a stop a hundred yards down the rails. The mule pulling the buggy had miraculously survived; the farmer driving the wagon hadn't been so lucky. Pete had often wondered what the driver had felt when the train hit him. Now, he had a pretty good idea.

The Pecos dust swallowed him, and the arena went black.

Chapter Two

He came to with a start, jerking himself up, the scent of animal sweat and manure heavy upon him, and a leathery black hand gripped his shoulder and stopped his progress.

"Not so fast, Mr. Belissari," Sgt. Major Cadwallader said. "Best have a shot of this first."

Pete realized he had been laying on the uncomfortable plank that served as the bar in the former buffalo soldier's tent saloon. He swung his feet over the side, slowly, cautiously, daring not to risk passing out. Cadwallader held a tin cup. When Belissari took the proffered whiskey, he noticed his ripped white shirtsleeve and stained arm, realizing that it wasn't just the scent of animal sweat and manure upon him. He gulped down some forty-rod rotgut, spiked with pepper, gunpowder, tobacco juice, and strychnine. If slamming into Bad Temper hadn't killed him, this probably would. He choked, eyes watering, as the whiskey blazed a path down his throat and spread like grapeshot through his stomach.

"How's Poseidon?" he asked when he could speak again.

"Fine." The curt reply came from Hannah. Pete saw her standing across the tent, hands behind her back, lips tight, eyes angry.

"Your horse caught a bit of the bull's horn," Cadwallader added. "He's all right, though. Buddy Pecos is stitching up the wound with some fishing line."

With a sigh, Pete drained the rest of the whiskey and returned the empty mug to Cadwallader.

"The boy's fine, too, Petros," Hannah said tightly.

The whiskey suddenly made him lightheaded. Hannah was angry at him, and he couldn't figure out why. He looked at her briefly, and then his eyes moved down the tent. He saw the woman, a beautiful woman with fiery red hair in extravagant curls and soothing hazel eyes, a stunning lady in a light blue dress, trimmed with braid down the front as well as on the collar, cuffs and pockets, with a cashmere wrap despite the warmth of West Texas in July. A picture of a goddess. Perhaps the most beautiful lady he had ever seen. The woman smiled, moved forward and extended her right hand delicately.

Pete took the small, smooth hand awkwardly, not knowing if he should shake or kiss it. He opted to kiss it.

"I am Lady Guinevere," she said in a voice that sounded like London—not that Pete had ever been to

London, or met royalty—but he had run across his share of remittance men, Englishmen and other Europeans in Texas. "I must thank you with all my heart, kind sir, for saving my only son's life." She reached into her purse and withdrew a greenback.

He stopped her. "I can't, Miss . . . Lady Guinevere," he said. "I mean, put the money away. If I . . . I didn't . . . I mean anyone might could have done it, ma'am. I just, well, was the closest fella handy."

He realized he sounded like some dumb Texas waddie, an uncouth oaf instead of a college graduate who could read Homer in the original Greek.

Lady Guinevere smiled, leaned forward, and kissed his bruised forehead. He cringed, expecting pain, but felt none, just a soft, wet kiss.

"I am in your debt, kind sir. Now I must find Eugene so he can thank you properly. Please do not leave until I return." She nodded at Cadwallader, smiled once more at Pete, ignored Hannah, and left.

Pete looked at Cadwallader. "Wow," the stunned old soldier said.

Hannah had another word, one best not spoken in front of a lady such as Guinevere.

"Petros Belissari," she said, moving toward him. "You numskull. *How's Poseidon?* Pete, how could you? You asked about your horse before you asked about the boy! Of all the . . ."

Pete was on his feet, kneeling in front of Cadwallader's tent saloon and shaking hands with the little boy in the city suit while Lady What'shername showed off her perfect teeth in a gorgeous smile that just heightened the witch's beauty. Not that Hannah Scott thought of the Englishwoman as a witch.

"Goober, mister?" the lad asked, and this time Pete smiled, pulled a large goober pea from the bag, cracked the peanut with his teeth, ate the peanuts and tossed the shell aside. Hannah made a face. Goober peas were the most repulsive food she had ever put in her mouth. Even worse than okra.

"I like the soggy ones," the boy said. "I et 'em, shells and all."

Strange, Hannah thought, how Eugene lacked the refined accent of his mother. Still, she had to admit that the boy was cute as a button. Hannah always had a soft spot in her heart for children. The seven orphans she kept at her Wild Rose Ranch were a testament to that.

Gripping the sides of her dress, she knelt beside Pete and smiled at the boy. "How old are you, Eugene?" The boy held out his left hand, spreading his fingers. "I'm five years old."

"And what brings you to Pecos, Texas?"

"The general."

Hannah looked up at Lady Guinevere. "His father?"

The woman's stunning eyes glistened with tears and she turned away. Hannah swallowed. Oops. Almost secretively, the redhead pulled a handkerchief from her purse and dabbed her eyes before turning back, forcing a radiant smile. "No," she said softly. "No, just a friend, an escort. My William—Eugene's father— he died heroically with Captain Moriarity and all the others at the Battle of Ntombe Drift. William was a lieutenant in the Eightieth Regiment. Poor Eugene . . .

he never got to know him. And my poor William never got to see our only son."

"I'm sorry," Pete said.

"It's all right," she said.

Hannah glanced at the boy. She wanted to wipe Eugene's nose, but that was a mother's job. The kid held out his bag of peanuts, but Hannah shook her head. "Eugene," she began, "how would you like to meet our children? I have three girls and four boys who'd just love to play with you and show you around. And they'd probably like a goober."

The child nodded, and Hannah looked up at Lady Guinevere for permission. The woman stared at her incredulously.

"You?" she asked. "You have seven children?"

Pete answered. "Orphans. Hannah runs an orphanage in Fort Davis."

"Oh." The boy looked at his mother with pleading eyes, and the lady nodded. "Yes, Eugene. You may go. But, please, do not go into the corral anymore."

"Yes'm." The kid looked back at Pete. "But that was a good wreck, mister. I liked it. Couldn't planned it no better."

Pete seemed to be at a loss for words. At last he smiled, removed the kid's silly hat, and tussled his dark hair. "Glad you enjoyed it, Eugene. But let's not make a habit of it, all right?"

"Okey dokey."

Hannah took the boy's hand and led him toward the arena, only to realize her error. She was leaving Petros alone with that buxom beauty. Of course, she trusted Pete. He was her betrothed, even though they hadn't gotten around to setting a wedding date. And he had been with her, through good and bad, better and worse, since May of '84. Three years now. He had saved her life. She had saved his. He was an honest man, kind, intelligent, a hard worker, well-disciplined. Certainly not a saint, but a good person, righteous and dependable.

But it would be a cold Fourth of July in Pecos City, Texas, before she ever trusted the likes of Lady Guinevere.

"Buddy," she called out, seeing the tall Texan with the thinning hair and dusty clothes. Good old Buddy Pecos, another good friend. The unreconstructed Rebel, back from stitching up Poseidon's wounds, shifted the bulging chaw in his mouth uncomfortably, shuffling his feet, not knowing what to expect. "Buddy, dear Buddy, would you be so kind as to take Eugene here and introduce him to Paco, Angelica, and everyone?"

"Yes, ma'am," Pecos answered, although Hannah could see the discomfort on his face. His one cold eye studied the skirt that came with the boy's blue suit. Hannah's orphan girls, Cynthia, Angelica, and Darcy, wore skirts. But the boys, Chris, Desmond, Bruce, and Paco, wouldn't be caught dead in such an outfit. Of course, what did Hannah know about fashion, stuck out here in spartan West Texas, four hundred and forty-one miles from San Antonio, two hundred and thirty-two miles from El Paso, two thousand miles from New York City? Maybe back east five-year-old boys wore skirts with their suits, but out here their Sunday-go-to-meeting clothes included stiff hand-me-down shoes, washed hand-me-down woolen pants, a boiled white shirt and a string tie, and a hand-me-down coats in fall and winter.

"Goober, mister?" Eugene asked Pecos as, hand in hand, they walked away.

Pete stood closer to the Englishwoman, smiling pleasantly, forgetting the blood matted on his dark mustache and walnut-sized knot on his forehead. He had taken a hard spill when Poseidon rammed the charging bull. She had admired his bravery. If not for him, Eugene might be dead, Julian Cale would likely be facing a lynch mob for introducing bullriding to the Pecos rodeo and Lady Guinevere would be sobbing uncontrollably and . . . hmmmm . . . on her way back east? Hannah bit her lip for such a wicked thought.

She put on a smile herself, and sidled up to Pete, taking his arm in her own. She would be sociable, polite, yet letting this English dame know Petros Belissari was private property. Trespassers shot on sight. Besides, tomorrow would find Pete and her back in the Davis Mountains, and Lady Guinevere and Eugene traveling somewhere else—Canada perhaps—with this "general."

"So you'll be in Fort Davis?" Pete was asking her.

"Yes." The woman smiled. She had such full lips. Hannah tried not to fume. "The general says it is the most wonderful town in all of Texas."

Pete nodded. "Well, the town isn't much—not compared to New York, or Austin for that matter—but the Davis Mountains are beautiful. And you'll find the weather cooler than out here on the Pecos, the scenery wonderful."

"Perhaps we can dine tomorrow evening in town?"

"Yes, ma'am . . ."

"Please, Mr. Belissari. Call me Guinevere."

"All right, Guinevere. But you must call me Pete."

It took all of Hannah's facial muscles to maintain that smile.

"Belissari . . . that is . . . Greek?"

She felt Pete's body straighten, impressed. "Yes, it is. But I'm first-generation American, born and reared in Corpus Christi. My father was a fisherman and sailor in the old country. He came to America in '51. Now he's captain of his own ship on the Texas coast."

"Delightful."

How nice, Hannah thought, for Pete to tell this stranger his life story. She realized Lady Guinevere's attention had turned to her. "And you?"

"Scott," Hannah said, trying not to sound snide. "It's Scottish, Lady Guinevere."

The fancy trollop laughed. "You Americans. I love your humor. Please, Miss Scott, I wish for you to call me Guinevere also. I'm not in England, so let us do away with those proper formalities."

"Call me Hannah." Somehow, she managed to get the words out and not choke.

"This is most excellent. Perhaps, I can talk our friend the general into hiring you, Pete, as our guide through this most wonderful country."

Pete nodded. "Well, who is this general, Lady . . . I mean, Guinevere? And what exactly what are you doing out here?"

As if on cue, a man clapped his hands and thundered out, "By jingo! I knew that had to be my old friend, Pete Belissari, when I saw that dashing display of Texas bravery, charging forward on his fine gray steed, fearless—by that I refer to both man and beast—riding headlong for glory and perhaps death simply to save the life of an innocent child. Never shirking in his duty, slamming into the side of a five-ton dragon of a terror like some self-propelled torpedo. *Wham!* The bull was knocked asunder, rising, turning its anger toward this fantastic man and horse—of course, the man had been catapulted like a fiery ball from a Roman candle, fitting on the day on which our country celebrates her independence. And next, before I could blink my eyes, came the other supporting characters in this real-life play staged before an appreciative audience. The stalwart Buddy Pecos, galloping his steady animal, and scooping up the young child to lead him out of Death's path. Another cowboy whom I have just interviewed, who roped the stunned bull just in the nick of time. And Cowboy Christopher, the brightest star in this bullriding event, dragging the unconscious Pete Belissari to safety.

"Splendid, it was. Capital. A most excellent scene to witness firsthand. It shall be the topic of my next Five Cent Wide Awake Library classic piece of literature, soon to be available by mail subscription or at your better mercantiles throughout this country."

The man, clad in beaded white buckskins despite the heat and a white hat with towering crown and massive brim, stuck out a meaty right paw. "Pete, my dearest friend, how great it is to see you again."

They shook, Pete once more speechless, and the

man tipped his hat at Hannah. "And the beauty of West Texas, Hannah. It has been much too long."

Hannah smiled. "It's good to see you, Colonel," she said.

"It's General, now, my dear. Brigadier General L. Merryweather Handal, esquire, noted scribe of the plains, friend to the noble red man, recorder of truth and real-life adventures, and, now, escort to a company of dignitaries and the cream of society, giving them a glimpse of our vanishing frontier. I see you have both met Lady Guinevere."

Handal smacked his lips. "I dare say, my fine friends, are they serving cocktails in that tent behind you?"

Chapter Three

Brig. Gen. L. Merryweather Handal sported a walrus mustache these days, with thick brown hair and a monocle over his left eye. They had first met, personally, in the fall of '85 near the silver-mining town of Shafter, south of Fort Davis between Marfa and Presidio. Of course, Pete and Hannah had been familiar with the honorable colonel's—er, general's—reputation long before then. Young Paco, now nine years old, had an insatiable taste for the flimsily written and packaged half-dime and dime novels churned out frequently by New York publishing houses.

And the honorable L. Merryweather Handal had become one of Paco's favorite storytellers despite Hannah's attempts to interest him in Charles Dickens, Alexandre Dumas, Jules Verne, James Fenimore Cooper, Bret Harte, and Mark Twain.

No luck. After all, how could titles like *Oliver Twist, The Three Musketeers, Journey to the Center of the Earth, Leatherstocking Tales, The Outcasts of Poker Flat*, and *The Prince and the Pauper* compare to *Plomo, The Terrible; or, The Masked Rider of Mexico . . . Plomo's Revenge; or, Mayhem in Old Monterrey . . . Wild Times in Wichita; or, An Ace for the Black Widow . . . This Man Colter; or, Harrowing Adventures of the Texas Borderman and His Belle*; and, the latest, *Buddy Pecos and the Greek Gun; or, True Adventures of Two Stalwart Texicans*?

Paco certainly loved Handal's glorification of Pete and Buddy, even if no one around Fort Davis could recognize one iota of truth in the slim novel.

Handal was forty-seven, would turn forty-eight next month, and had worked for several Western newspapers before turning to write five-penny dreadfuls. He had been married, and divorced, four times, found his career teetering on oblivion, but enjoyed a glorious rebirth when he came to West Texas, wound up saving Pete's life, as well as Hannah's, and ending a "homely dominion of obdurate tumult and consternation"—his words, not Hannah's—by helping capture or kill the gangs of Plomo and Cochrane Smith, two of the most notorious bandits in the Big Bend.

He was back, God bless him, bringing supper guests to the Wild Rose Ranch. European royalty. Lady Guinevere and her son. Others Hannah hadn't met. She wiped sweat from her brow and continued to peel potatoes in the cook shed behind her small cabin.

Back in Pecos, Pete had talked the colonel—er, general—into stopping here for supper. After all, the ranch sat on the San Antonio–El Paso Road, bordering Limpia Creek and just below Wild Rose Pass, a mere ten miles from the town of Fort Davis and the sprawling military post where soldiers of the Third and Eight U.S. Cavalry and Sixteenth U.S. Infantry were garrisoned. Hannah had expected Merryweather Handal and Lady Guinevere to decline the hospitality, preferring a cozy bed at the Hotel Limpia or Stewart's Hotel instead of pitching tents on the ranch or sleeping in the barn. Yet the incorrigible writer clapped his hands, shouted, "Capital!" and agreed.

So Hannah found herself brewing tea and cooking supper for—how many people did Handal say?—fifteen.

Fifteen!

Plus the seven kids of her own, herself, Pete, Buddy, and their hired hand, Irwin Sawyer. Well, she didn't know if European dignitaries and the "cream of society" liked mashed potatoes, fried steak, and biscuits, but that's what they were getting. Nor would they be served champagne or good wines. Out here, tea was a luxury, so they were lucky to get that. Or they could help themselves to strong, bitter coffee or cool well water. And if they wanted something stronger . . . well, knowing the honorable L. Merryweather Handal, he had already procured some of Milton Faver's peach brandy. Hannah could use a shot of the aging don's liquor herself just about now.

Pete stuck his head in the door. "Need any help?"

"No, thanks," she lied, and wiped her brow with the back of her arm.

"Well, they're topping the pass right now."

She took a deep breath. Already here.

"You've never seen the likes of this, Hannah," he continued. "Three covered wagons, one chuckwagon, a remuda and three military ambulances."

"You sure it's them?" She held out some hope.

"Our friend General Handal, resplendent in his buckskins, is leading the way on a black horse."

"Great. And what's Lady Guinevere riding?"

"Didn't see her." He seemed excited as Paco before going to town, not detecting the sarcasm in her voice. "Imagine she's in one of the ambulances. I'll greet our guests, get the corrals ready for their horse herd."

He left.

Hannah nicked her thumb with the knife, and stopped short of muttering an oath. Peach brandy? Nah, right now she'd welcome some of Cadwallader's scamper juice.

Pete recognized the tall, thin driver of the lead wagon immediately. Good old David Goldman. A native of Missouri, Goldy and Pete had worked together back in '85 when they operated the Argo Stagecoach Company. Goldman had run a stage station down in Shafter with Happy Jack McBride, but after they sold the stage line, which was now out of business, McBride and Goldman also sold their claim. Happy Jack was now touring with Buffalo Bill Cody's Wild West, and the last time Pete had seen David Goldman, he was leaving West Texas for the civilization of Dallas.

"Good to see you," Pete said, after Goldy set the brake and climbed off the wagon.

"Likewise."

"Miss us, or was Dallas too big for you?"

Goldy shrugged. "Nope, nothing like that. Handal and his entourage just came through Dallas and started hiring. Fifty a month for driving a wagon, Pete, and this is one posh setup, my friend."

Belissari couldn't argue there. A small, dark-bearded man with black eyes drove the second wagon, and a leathery guy, as thin as a fence post dressed in greasy buckskins and chewing tobacco, pulled back the brake on the third wagon. Pete looked closer. That wasn't a man, but a woman. A towering black man with a spade beard parked the chuckwagon, and a Mexican *vaquero* herded the horses into the corral before Irwin Sawyer and Buddy Pecos shut the gate.

Then came the ambulances. The first was driven by a wiry gent in dirty homespun clothes and spectacles, with Lady Guinevere looking strikingly lovely in a green dress, and not a speck of dust upon her clothes despite the long ride from Pecos. Beside her sat Eugene, his face clean for once, hands (not holding a bag of peanuts) folded behind his head, which still sported that silly-looking hat.

A young man in a broadcloth suit and Abe Lincoln hat drove the next ambulance, with a middle-aged couple in beautiful clothes as passengers. The last wagon was driven by an olive-skinned, raven-haired lady in a navy blue dress, with two men sitting behind her, one of them wearing a spiked dress helmet and military uniform with French braid.

Trailing the group came a lone rider, a leathery man in need of a shave, with matted sandy hair blowing in the wind, a black Spanish hat hanging on his back held by a horsehair latigo string, and linen duster protecting most of his clothes, but the right tail tucked behind his gunbelt.

"Peter, it's grand to see you."

Belissari smiled at Merryweather Handal. "We'll get on with introductions, my good friend," the writer said, "but first I wonder if I might impose on you, good lad, to help me down from this towering beast?"

Baron Van Hallstedt clicked his heels and bowed slightly, tucking the dress helmet underneath his left arm. "It is a pleasure, Miss Scott." He took Hannah's hand and brought it to his lips. "Please allow me to introduce my associate, Herr Dr. Ludwig Schnitzler of Vienna."

Van Hallstedt, whom Handal said had been a hero of the Franco-Prussian War, was a short man even in his high-heeled military boots. His accent and features were harsh, although his attire—and that of his companion—were splendid. Hannah curtsied to the baron and smiled at the tall doctor, dressed in a black suit with tails, with blue eyes and a neatly trimmed mustache. The doctor also took Hannah's hand and kissed it gently, bowing gracefully but saying nothing.

"And the lady with you . . ." Hannah looked around, couldn't see the stunning young woman who had been driving the ambulance. Driving? What were these gentlemen doing letting a woman drive a wagon?

"Bonaventura?" Van Hallstedt's tone seemed bewildered. "Our servant?"

Hannah didn't know what to say, so she smiled, curtsied once more, and moved down the line.

"And this, Hannah," Handal said, "is Col. Gustave Klint, his wife, Dagmar, and son Carl, also of Vienna."

The son, a handsome lad probably in his early twenties, had been driving his parents. They seemed like a nice family, and Hannah liked them a lot more than she did Van Hallstedt and Dr. Schnitzler when they simply shook her hand rather than kissed it. Besides, she didn't feel as though she had to bow to these, and they didn't have a woman servant driving their ambulance.

"Of course, you know Lady Guinevere and Master Eugene already."

Hannah smiled. Guinevere didn't.

"And this dashing fellow is my associate, Mr. Butterworth."

He ran his hands through his curly hair, wet with sweat, and pulled on his black hat simply so he could tug at the brim.

Butterworth smiled. Hannah didn't.

There was something about him that she didn't like. Maybe it was the heavy smell of tobacco smoke on his breath. Maybe the way he carried himself like some strutting gamecock. More than likely it was how he wore the ivory-handled Colt on his right hip. A gunman. Or at least that's how he fancied himself.

"My pleasure, Mr. Butterworth."

They walked past the outside table, covered with a checkered cloth and plenty of food and drink. "Of course, Hannah," Handal went on, "I have saved my favorite introduction for last." He put thumb and forefinger in his mouth and let loose with a whistle that almost ruptured Hannah's eardrums.

A tall figure in dirty buckskins and an ugly hat, after spraying the children's mutt of a dog with tobacco juice, smiled and sprinted across the yard and leaped into Handal's arms, almost knocking the self-styled general to the ground. They spun around, and the man—no, a woman!—giggled and planted a wet smooch on Handal's cheek, staining his skin with a brown impression of her thin lips.

"Hannah," Handal said, dropping the woman to her feet, and trying to catch his breath. "This is my wife, Jones."

The woman spit into her right hand and stuck it at Hannah. "Put'r there, lady. I's heard an awful lot about you, and any ol' friend of L. Merryweather here is a dandy ol' friend of mine."

Reluctantly, Hannah shook the woman's bony, calloused hand. Afterward, she tried to wipe her hand on her apron without offending Handal's bride.

"Jones?" Hannah asked. "An interesting name."

"Jones. Yep. Jones Handal is now me handle." She cackled. "Well, Smith was already a-taken." She tugged on her hat brim. "Mighty glad to know you, Miss Hannah. Yessirreebob, mighty glad." Jones Handal turned to her husband. "See you later, honey-dumplins. Gotta check on the stock."

After eating, Handal took his guests to show them around the ranch, Buddy Pecos and Irwin Sawyer in tow, while Paco, Cynthia, and the other children tried to introduce Eugene to the sport of baseball. Hannah had started to clear the table of dishes when she looked across the yard and realized those servants and drivers hadn't eaten. Well, she had cooked enough food for them, so she nodded at Pete and crossed the yard. Pete followed.

The black man with the thick beard looked up and smiled after tearing off a hunk of jerky with his teeth. "Hello," Hannah said and introduced herself. "Listen, there's plenty of food to go around. I didn't realize y'all hadn't eaten until now. Please, help yourself."

The man rose, shaking his head. "No thank you, ma'am. We'll be fine."

"I insist," Hannah said.

The chuckwagon driver looked at the others: the lovely woman who had driven Van Hallstedt's and Doctor Schnitzler's wagon; the black-haired *vaquero* in charge of the remuda; the bespectacled man who had driven Lady Guinevere and Eugene; David Goldman; the black-bearded wagon driver; even Handal's wife, Jones.

Pete stepped forward, and offered his hand. "Pete Belissari," he said. "Come on. Out here, we don't let food go to waste. And Hannah's a good cook, I can assure you."

David Goldman smiled. "I can vouch for that. And our cook up and quit on us back at Fort Stockton. Let's eat." Goldy didn't wait for the others.

The black man shook Pete's hand. "I'm Tom Rockwall," he said. He eyed Hannah. "This is mighty nice of you, ma'am."

"Call me Hannah."

Rockwall nodded at the others. Jones Handal cut loose with a Rebel yell, hooked the chaw of tobacco from of her mouth with a thumb, and sprinted across the yard.

The *vaquero* bowed slightly. "*Me lama Ramón Armando. Muchas gracias, señorita.*"

"*De nada,*" said Hannah.

Lady Guinevere's driver tried to clean the lenses of his glasses with a dirty bandana. "Call me Nehemiah," he said finally. "Thanks for your hospitality, folks. Sure could use some good grub."

That left only the black-haired man. He considered Hannah briefly before straightening his shoulders and stepping in front of Pete. "Is this your woman?" he asked. The accent was strange, perhaps European.

Pete suddenly frowned. He didn't answer.

"Bee-liss-ah-ree," the swarthy man went on. "That is your name?"

"Yes," he answered tightly.

The driver spat at Pete's moccasins. "I'll eat no food served by a woman of yours, you Greek fiend."

Pete's fist came up quickly and slammed into the little man's jaw, decking him.

"You Turkish son of—"

He didn't finish. Instead, he dove on top of the wagon driver.

Chapter Four

"It's the mother lode," L. Merryweather Handal kept saying, between sips from a brown clay jug and diatribes on his latest business venture. Pete and Buddy Pecos sat among the shade trees behind the main cabin, waiting for the dime novelist to share the peach brandy, but the honorable general never let the jug pass his hands. Belissari rubbed his skinned knuckles, only half-listening to the monologue, recalling the short-lived fight against that miserable Turk.

Pecos and Irwin Sawyer had pulled Pete off the runt before Belissari had worked up much of a sweat. And when the wagon driver sneered after being helped to his feet by Hannah, Pete sent the heels of his moccasins into the Turk's chest, propelling the lowdown snake into the hard rails of the corrals. That had been quite satisfying until Hannah began railing till her ears turned beet red and she lost her breath. Finally, she managed to get Jones Handal and Tom Rockwall to carry the battered man to the cabin so she could clean him up, bandage the cuts, and maybe put some raw meat on that blackened eye. She had given Pete a scowl that he interpreted rather quickly and correctly: *And then, Mister, I'm gonna rip your head off for attacking one of our guests.*

An hour later, she met Pete in his room off the barn, although she had calmed down enough to listen to his explanation.

"Pete, I've been insulted before," she said afterward. "You don't have to defend my honor just because some loco wagon driver . . . besides, 'a woman of yours' isn't exactly the same as a trollop or soiled dove. And you've been called worse than a 'Greek fiend'."

"You don't understand," he said.

"I guess I don't."

"He's Turkish."

She stared without comprehension.

Belissari sighed. "The Ottoman empire and Greece do not get along. Haven't for centuries. And he started it!"

"*He started it?* Pete, he never got in a punch." Belissari tried not to smile or gloat over his victory. Hannah would tear his head off if he didn't look the least bit humble.

"He would have attacked, the sneaky louse."

"Pete!" She sighed. "Why? Explain to me this, this feud if you will, between Greeks and Turks. Then maybe I can understand."

Explain? He shook his head. That's like asking an Apache to say why he hates Mexicans, or a Sioux to justify the tribe's bloody discord with the Crow. It's like asking Buddy Pecos to say why he still despises Yankees more than twenty years after the War, the Suttons to explain their feud with the Taylors, or the Irish to describe the injustices done at the English's hands. Greeks didn't like Turks. Never had. Never would. The Ottoman Empire was evil. Always had been. Always would be.

Shaking her head, Hannah, exasperated, left him alone.

"I'll pay you one hundred and fifty dollars a month."

That got Pete's attention. He stared at L. Merryweather Handal and let his brain catch up on whatever it had been the colonel—er, general—had been talking about.

"I tell you boys, it's the mother lode," the writer reiterated. "These European dudes, dandies, dudeesses and dandy-esses, they just love the glory of the American frontier, the West, the *Wild* West, and they are willing to pay good money for a chance to live the lives of my heroes in print. By Jupiter, they can't get enough of it. And, quite naturally, I, Brigadier General L. Merryweather Handal, do not forget my friends and am happy to share my splendid fortunes. What say you gents?"

Buddy Pecos answered first after scratching his beard stubble on his chin. "The last time a body offered me that kind of cash money, he wanted me to do some things with my Big Fifty that the law frowns upon."

Handal roared with laughter, careful not to spill his peach brandy. "Fear not, my stalwart Texas champion. What I need from you is your sharpshooting prowess, but you will not be aiming at living human beings . . ." His voice trailed off, and he looked into the trees, lost in thought. After several seconds, he continued. "Unless . . . maybe . . . by Jove, my customers would love to be ambushed by merciless red savages, their faces painted black with hatred, vowing with blood to drive all white settlers from this country that had been their own long before alligators and dinosaurs ruled the earth, wailing like banshees with their tremendous war cries. Yes. Yes. And then you, lean, leathery, whip snapper of a gunman Buddy Pecos. You, with your trusty rifle and keen eyes—I mean eye, sorry—you drive them off by shooting true, true, true." He clapped his hand. "That's it. Where can we find some savage Sioux?"

Buddy and Pete glanced at each other before staring at a beaming General Handal.

"Try Dakota Territory," Pete suggested.

"On the reservations," Pecos added.

"A thousand miles from here," Pete said.

Handal shook his head, not detecting their teasing. "Too far," he said softly. "Much too far. What is the most fiendish tribe roaming these parts?"

"The crib girls in Chihuahua Town," Pecos suggested, slapping his knee.

"There must be some noble red men that can attack my customers," Handal said.

Pete shook his head. "General, the Comanches are on the reservation in the Indian Nations. The Mescaleros are in New Mexico. And I'm not sure your paying customers would really want to be jumped by Comanches or Apaches. Trust me."

After another pull on the jug, Handal solemnly agreed and dismissed the thought of an Indian attack. "Anyway," he began, speeding up his sentences, eyes full of excitement once more, "I'd like to hire you both as guides for one hundred and fifty a month, most likely for a month, no more than two. Buddy Pecos, you'll be our glorious hunter, a guide to take Baron Van Hallstedt, Gustave Klint and Carl, and Ludwig Schnitzler to seek out the giant game in these splendid but quaint mountains. Elk. Antelope. Coyotes and wolves. Cougars. The ferocious grizzly with his giant paws of death, capable of eviscerating man or beast with one quick slash of those diabolic claws."

Antelope and cougars probably, Pete thought. Gray wolves still preyed on the occasional calf, and coyotes were as common as jack rabbits. But elk were few, and grizzlies had been driven or killed out of the country although a hunter could come across a black bear in the mountains, not that he'd want to.

"What do I do?" Belissari asked.

The self-commissioned general slammed a cork into the jug and pulled himself to his feet, swaying a little bit after several swallows of peach brandy. "You, Pete Belissari—" Handal belched—"the fearless, daring horseman of the Davis Mountains? Well, sir, you'll help guide our merry crew across these broken hills that look majestic and purple but can be savage and

full of black death so cruel, heartless and cold. And
the great baron has a hankering to catch wild mustangs
and break one for his very own. That's your depart-
ment, Peter. Speaking of which, I asked that broken-
down rancher Cale to bring by a horse here tomorrow
morning for an exhibition. Rest up, Peter, for the lights
will be shining on you then in our corral."

"What?"

Handal didn't answer. "Afterward, we shall depart
for parts unknown, for our European visitors to see the
true West of these United States of America, to see
what we have learned after two hundred years of independence from the bloody English."

"It's a hundred and eleven years, General," Pete
corrected.

"Well, now," Handal said, "I must go find my
lovely wife and entertain our guests. Then we're off,
Bud and Peter, to find glory, adventure, and money,
money, money. By the way, if one of you fine gentlemen knows where we can also hire a cook, I'll pay
seventy-five a month. And Peter, dear friend, please I
beg of you to cease and desist your violent persecution
of my wagon driver."

Pete had explained everything perfectly. The money
offered by Handal was too good to pass up. A hundred
and fifty dollars a month? It would take most men in
West Texas three to five months to earn those kind of
wages. Chris and Irwin could handle the chores around
the ranch, work the cattle and everything. Pete would
be back in a month, no more than two, with money to
put in the coffers, maybe buy the kids some new

clothes and shoes. With a smile, he even promised he wouldn't strangle the Ottoman wagon driver although Hannah suspected sweet Petros had crossed his fingers behind his back.

All he had to do was lead the group into the mountains, try to find a mustang herd to please Baron Van Hallstedt, maybe show them the Indian drawings, do a little hunting, some entertainment, maybe even guide them into the Chinanti Mountains way down south and take them to Don Flannan's baronial fort for some of *Señora* Luz's *frijoles*, enchiladas, and chili con queso for a respite before putting Merryweather and his merry crew on the first eastbound train in Marfa and heading home.

As soon as Merryweather hired a cook they'd be on their way. The quicker they got started, the faster Pete would be home.

It sounded fine. They certainly could use the money. Not that Petros Belissari needed Hannah's blessing or permission to do anything he wanted. They weren't married—yet—though there was an understanding that someday, when they had enough cash put away, when things finally settled down, when they could find time to rope a preacher . . .

She was about to say "fine," when Darcy opened the door and led a stunning, lush Lady Guinevere inside. "Hi, Mama Hannah," the child said. "I'm showing Lady Guinevere my dolly."

The woman gave Pete and Hannah a smile and allowed herself to be pulled to Darcy's small bed, where a moth-eaten rag doll Hannah had made some time ago rested on a flat pillow. The English strumpet sat on the edge of the bed, and Darcy handed her the toy.

"Why, she is the most precious doll I have ever seen," Guinevere said in a high-pitched voice. "What's her name?"

"Dolly."

"That's a nice name."

"You want to see my dead grasshopper?"

"Certainly."

Hannah pursed her lips. Darcy Comhghall hated strangers, yet she had immediately been attracted to Lady Guinevere. It had taken Hannah months to crack the orphan's shell, and she had never once offered to show Hannah a dead grasshopper. Hannah didn't even know the kid had put the dead insect in a small wooden box—and she lived in the same house, tucked Darcy and the others (except Christopher, who claimed he was too old) in bed every night.

"Do you know what, Darcy?" Guinevere asked, admiring the insect.

"What?"

"I bet my son would love to see your pet grasshopper. I don't think he has ever seen a grasshopper before."

"All right!" Darcy said, and bolted out the house, screaming Eugene's name and slamming the door behind her.

Lady Guinevere stood, looking like she had been dressed, bathed, and pampered by twenty servants, her red curls perfect, lips bright, not even a trace of sweat or discomfort, yellow dress revealing her perfect body, and that smile, that bright, wicked, miserable, pathetic little smile.

"What a charming little girl," the witch said. "You must be proud."

"She can be a handful," Pete said. "Coffee?"

"Please."

Guinevere made herself at home, sitting at the table, noticing the uneven legs on the chair as well as the uneven floor. She said nothing, and complimented Pete on the coffee. Of course, Hannah had made the coffee, ground the beans, boiled the water, added the sugar, and given the peppermint stick that came in the Arbuckles can to Darcy.

Darcy the traitor.

Hannah was aware of her windblown hair, her face damp with sweat, dirty from cleaning and cooking, her own worn clothes. She had a dress like the one Lady Guinevere wore—well, maybe it cost thirty dollars less, maybe it needed ironing, yeah, the cuffs were frayed, and . . . well, it was the same color—and if she got her hair curled, had a nice, cool bath and some. . . . She let out a silent sigh. Nope. She couldn't look that way if she had a thousand servants and two thousand dollars.

"I hear you are coming with us, Petros," Lady Perfect said.

"Looks that way," Pete said, daring not to face Hannah now.

"Marvelous."

Lady Guinevere turned to Hannah. "And you, Miss Scott. Are you coming, too?"

The thought came to Hannah quickly. It surprised her that she hadn't thought of it before.

"Of course," she answered. "Pete says y'all need a cook."

Chapter Five

Hannah had explained everything perfectly. The money offered by General Handal was too good to pass up. Seventy-five dollars a month? That's better than what most top cooks made on ranches in West Texas. Chris and Irwin could handle the chores around the ranch, look after the children and everything. They would be back in a month, no more than two, with even more money for clothes, food, shoes. Maybe they could fix up the cabin some. With a smile, she even promised she would look after Petros, to make sure he wasn't ambushed by the Ottoman wagon driver.

Or Lady Guinevere, she told herself.

And the honorable Brig. Gen. L. Merryweather Handal found it a "capital!" idea.

So it was settled.

The following morning after breakfast, Julian Cale

rode in with a couple of his cowboys and a fifteen-hand mustang stallion widowmaker that needed his humps ironed out. Apparently, Lady Guinevere, Baron Van Hallstedt, and the travelers from Vienna hadn't gotten enough of the Pecos rodeo, so Handal informed Pete that his first job would be to put on a bronc-busting exhibition. "That cow-riding was fine, simply fine," Handal told him, "but it will never please the spectators like a good cowboy trying to tame a magnificent thoroughbred."

"It was a bull, not a cow," Belissari corrected. "There's a big difference." He didn't bother to explain the difference between a mustang and a thoroughbred.

Pete sat on his cot, stuffing an extra shirt and some socks into his warbag along with *The Iliad*, shaving kit, and kidskin gloves. He had cleaned and loaded the Winchester carbine as well as the Colt revolver holstered in his shellbelt. He placed the canvas bag beside the weapons, pulled his hat down, and headed for the door just as Gen. L. Merryweather Handal barged in.

"The guests are waiting, my boy! Hustle, lad, hustle."

"I'm ready," Pete said and started forward, but Handal grabbed his shoulder. Belissari faced the hack writer, who smiled and gestured toward the horseman's waist.

"Peter, aren't you a bit undressed?"

Belissari waited for an explanation. Handal tilted his neck toward the cot. Pete still didn't understand.

"Your revolver, boy. You're a man of the West, son, and my customers expect to see you heeled, strapping a big iron on your hip, a tool for some, a lethal instrument of death for others, the great equalizer invented by Mr. Thomas Colt."

"Sam Colt," Pete said and smiled. "I'm going to ride a bronc, General. Not shoot it."

"Nonetheless, Peter, I insist that you strap on that deadly six-shooter." Handal's eyes lighted on the coat rack where a fringed buckskin jacket hung. "And that coat, sir. Yes. Absolutely. You must wear that buckskin. By Jupiter, that's a brilliant idea."

Belissari let out a half-sigh, half-laugh. "General," he began, "it's a little warm for that jacket. This is July, sir."

"Poppycock. You, sir, are starting to sound ungrateful, a mite insubordinate, and I needn't remind you, Peter, that my rank is general and you are a mere civilian. And lest you forget, son, that it is I, the honorable Brigadier General L. Merryweather Handal, esquire, noted scribe of the plains, who is paying you one hundred and fifty dollars a month. The coat, my dear lad, and the ruinous revolver."

With a sigh, Belissari buckled on the gunbelt, the holster high on his right hip, but Handal shook his head violently and said, "No, no, no, no. You must wear the gun low on your hip, for an easy pull. Fancy yourself as another Mr. Butterworth, cold-blooded killer, gunman, quicker than greased lightning with that terrible, wonderful bit of five-pound blue steel."

Pete did as he was told, although the Colt felt awkward resting so low. At least it didn't weigh five pounds as Handal said. More like two or three. He pulled on the buckskin jacket and stood awaiting L. Merryweather Handal's approval.

"Perfect, dear boy. By jingo, you could be a model for the cover of my next Five Cent Wide Awake Library masterpiece." He walked forward and put his arm around Belissari's shoulder, saying in a soothing tone as they walked out the door: "Remember, what my guests want to see is the mythical, magical West. Think about that great piece of Greek literature, *Beowulf*. Think of Balzac's *The Three Musketeers*. Adventure! Daring deeds. Then put them in a border setting. You are now a thespian, Peter Belissari, and I am giving you your greatest role."

Hannah snickered at Pete's costume as he ducked inside the corral where Cale's cowboys had the widowmaker waiting for him. The taller of the waddies had thrown a coat over the mustang's head, blinding him, to calm him down.

"Here, ladies and gentlemen!" L. Merryweather Handal called out in a voice that needed no amplification. "Here is a true display of the great American West. *Mano a mano*. Man versus beast. A Texas cowboy matching wits against a wily steed. Of course, for a man like Peter Belissari, the deadly Greek Gun, this is nothing more than a chess match. . . ."

"That fool always talk that much?" the second cowboy asked.

"Yeah," Pete said, shunning his jacket and gunbelt and handing both to the cowhand. As soon as Belissari's left foot touched the stirrup, the first cowboy bit the mustang's ear, and Pete quickly hauled himself into the saddle. The jacket covering the black stallion's eyes was jerked off, and Pete began a jarring ride that lasted all of three seconds.

He rolled underneath the rails and sat up wheezing.

"Hope you can do better than that, pilgrim," someone said and expunged tobacco juice between Belissari's legs. Pete looked up and saw Jones Handal shaking her head and shifting the chaw of tobacco from one cheek to the other. "Thought you was some great horseman, fella. Shucks, I can ride better than that. How much is my honey-dumplins payin' you?"

On the second ride, Pete lasted fifteen seconds, giving Handal's customers something to cheer about, before the mustang tried to rake Pete's right leg against the corral, then went into a spinning move that left Belissari pulling leather for three or four bucks before he landed in the dust once more.

As Belissari dusted himself off, he heard Merryweather's voice: "Friends, don't be discouraged. As the saying in these parts goes, 'There is not a horse that cannot be ridden, and . . . and . . . and . . .' "

Julian Cale came to Handal's rescue: "Never was a horse that couldn't be rode, and never was a rider that couldn't be throwed."

"That's for certain!" Jones Handal chimed in, cackling.

It took four more tries before Pete rode the mustang to a standstill. Of course, Belissari knew it would take more rides to get the stallion used to saddle, bit, and rider. He remained green and skittish, definitely not ready for working cattle or a Sunday afternoon ride, but the Europeans seemed satisfied that, in Merryweather's words, "the hand of man has tamed the wild beast."

Pete wanted to find a pool in Limpia Creek and

wash off the cakes of dust and grime, but as soon as he stepped out of the corral, Handal had barked orders for him to don his gunbelt and jacket and prepare for another exhibition. They walked across the road where Jones Handal had propped several whiskey bottles, empty of course, on various boulders on the dry creek-bed.

"Out on the border," the dime novelist began, "the blink of the eye can be the difference between life and death. Steely nerves are required when you face gun-men, cutthroats, rogues, and thieves. So, now, The Greek Gun, Peter Belissari, Buddy Pecos, and Mr. Butterworth will perform an exhibition displaying their mastery as shootists."

Belissari had dragged himself across the road. His throat felt raw, parched, yet no one had offered him a drink of water. And now the honorable L. Merry-weather Handal told him to go first, explaining how The Greek Gun would jerk the deadly Colt from its holster, cock, and fire in one swift motion almost too fast for the human eye to observe. With a thunderous clap, Handal boomed, "*Draw!*"

And Pete, too tired to think straight, drew. Only the holster came up with the revolver all the way to his waist before he managed to get the Colt clear. He heard Julian Cale's snickers as he thumbed back the hammer, fired . . . and missed.

He looked at the smoking barrel as if it had been the gun's fault. He stared at the targets, pretty far away, likely out of pistol range. He looked at the frowning crowd until his eyes locked on Lady Guin-evere. Just like that, he cocked the Colt, aimed and fired again. The bullet whined off a rock, kicking up dust about three yards in front of the closest whiskey bottle. Pete jerked back the hammer once more, and steadied himself. He had never been a great shot with a handgun, and wouldn't call himself a marksman with a rifle. But he was better than some with both. At least, that's what he told himself.

The Colt bucked, and the glass shattered. Belissari holstered the revolver, pleased at himself, and saw Lady Guinevere cheering loudly. Pete couldn't help but smile. Hannah, he noticed, wasn't smiling.

"Pathetic," L. Merryweather Handal whispered. "You'd be dead now if those bottles were shooting back."

"Twenty-five yards is a pretty far target for a short gun," Pete argued.

That comment brought a mirthless laugh from Mr. Butterworth, who quickly whipped out his revolver. Six shots echoed in rapid succession, obliterating Handal's partner's face with smoke. With the smoke cleared, a smiling Mr. Butterworth spun the pistol on his finger and eased the gun into the holster, slick with hog grease. Pete looked at the creekbed. Four more bottles had been broken.

"Four of six!" Gustave Klint exclaimed. "That is great shooting. Bravo!"

Now, Buddy Pecos hefted his Big Fifty. For show, he picked up a handful of dirt and let it sift through his fingers. "Always check for wind," he told the crowd. Not that it mattered, Pete thought. Shooting a .50-caliber rifle at a glass target twenty-five yards away . . . Heck, the concussion alone would probably break the bottle. And there was no wind.

Handal began: "I ask you to picture in your minds the great herds of buffalo that once grazed our American prairies. Millions of them. But men like the great Buddy Pecos of Texas. They helped put buffalo tongue on your tables. Imagine the smell of buffalo rump roasting over an open prairie. Imagine the hides of these glorious beasts being shipped to places like Dodge City and New York and, yes, even London or Vienna. Imagine the noble red man fighting to preserve his way of life." He clapped his hands loudly. "Suddenly, the buffalo runners are attacked by a party of warring Cherokees! But men like Buddy Pecos fear not the horrible fate awaiting them if they are caught by these fearless warriors. But fear not! For Buddy Pecos is armed with a tremendous Remington Rolling Block rifle, the same weapon that laid so many thousands of buffalo low, low, low."

"It's a Sharps," Pecos said, and pulled a trigger.

Handal leaped back, covering his ears, but the only sound coming from the rifle was a metallic click.

"Misfire?" Carl Klint asked.

"Double triggers," Pecos explained. "The first one sets it for firin'." He pulled the second trigger, and the Sharps rifle roared like a battery of cannon. The whiskey bottle practically disintegrated.

Little Eugene wailed, "Don't let him shoot that no more, Mama! I don't like it. It hurts my ears."

"Fantastic," Handal said, although he kept both forefingers plugged in his ears. "And now, we will head back across the road for warm food and cool drink before taking off for the mountains and rugged American adventure."

Jones Handal cocked her Winchester. "Not so fast," she said. "We got some targets that our fearless Greek Gun and Mr. Butterworth botched." The rifle popped, the bottles burst, and with a snicker, Jones Handal walked back toward the ranch yard.

Chapter Six

They didn't get far that first day. Baron Van Hallstedt and Ludwig Schnitzler demanded a chance for pistol lessons from Mr. Butterworth, Lady Guinevere had a hard time getting her son from the makeshift baseball field with the orphans, Colonel Gustave Klint demanded tea, Dagmar Klint pleaded that they postpone their departure until the heat had broken, and Carl Klint asked for a chance to ride Julian Cale's mustang—and was promptly thrown.

Finally, though, the wagon train got moving, pointed toward the southeastern part of the mountains. The party made camp early—it seems Herr Schnitzler wanted (demanded) some tea—and Hannah Scott found herself exhausted after cooking for first the Europeans and afterward for the servants and General Handal's hired help. Merryweather explained that she need not cook for the others, that the hired help could fend for themselves, but he cowered at Hannah's glare and said, "Suit yourself." Now she sat, her aching back resting against the chuckwagon's rear wheel, and dealt cards to Buddy, Pete, and Dave Goldman to pass the time. It seemed interesting, she thought, how the people separated into different cliques.

The good baron and the Vienna men sat outside a giant tent, with Merryweather entertaining them and describing the perils that could await the entire party. Bonaventura waited patiently for any orders such as refilling their coffee cups or fanning the cigar smoke from the men's faces. Mrs. Klint had retired alone, famished from the heat (not that Hannah thought it was hot), while Carl and Mr. Butterworth had gone exploring on their own and were doing a little target practice. The pops of Butterworth's revolver could be heard in the distance followed by Carl Klint's excited cheers. Inside their tent, Lady Guinevere sang a lullaby to Eugene. Dave Goldman commented on the Englishwoman's beautiful voice, but Pete had the brains not say anything, and especially knew better than to agree with David even though Hannah could not find one flaw with the redheaded soprano. Ramón the wrangler and the wagon drivers, the Turk, Nehemiah, and Tom Rockwall, sat on the opposite side of camp, drinking coffee and smoking cigarettes. And Jones Handal slept snoring beside the livestock.

Hannah looked at her cards and said, "Oh, my."

Goldman laughed. "Ain't rightly a poker face, ma'am," he said.

"She's bluffin'," Buddy commented and tossed one card onto the dirt. "Gimme one."

Goldman took three cards, and an exhausted Pete did the same. Hannah held three kings and pitched the ten of diamonds and seven of clubs. After dealing herself two cards, she asked, "Well?"

"Nothin'," Buddy said, turned his head to spit, and threw in his hand.

"Pair of fours," Goldman said meekly.

Pete shrugged and said, "Beats a pair of threes."

Hannah grinned excitedly. "I win," she said, and showed off her three kings, queen of diamonds, and ace of spades. She gathered up the cards to deal again.

"Glad we ain't playin' for money," Pecos said.

She dealt another round, still pleased, feeling like Hannah Scott, Woman Gambler, but Goldy reminded her she needed to deal everyone five cards, not four, and she pouted slightly and dealt each player another card.

"Where you plan on takin' these folks?" Pecos asked and took four cards.

Pete shrugged. "Make base camp the day after tomorrow near that spring and cave if we can get these wagons there. You can take them hunting, Mrs. Klint can enjoy the cool shade, and I'll see about setting up a corral trap higher up for any mustangs."

Dave Goldman asked for three cards. Pete also took three. Hannah held the nine of diamonds, eight of clubs, ten of diamonds, and queen of hearts. She remembered her poker lessons from Buddy, but she pitched the three anyway and drew the jack of spades to fill in her straight. Hannah won again, beating

Buddy's pair of twos, Goldman's pair of sevens, and Pete's pair of threes.

"You ought to set up a table at the Addition," Pecos commented.

Hannah gathered the cards and began to shuffle before realizing everyone was looking up behind her. She turned, her good mood suddenly soured by the presence of Lady Guinevere.

"You get your youngun to sleep?" Goldman asked.

"Yes," she said with a bright smile. "At last. He was so excited about the day, and cannot wait until tomorrow's further adventures." She sniffed the air. "What is that smell?"

Pete, Goldy, and Buddy exchanged looks, wondering if their clothes had soured in the heat. Hannah, however, recognized the musky odor immediately.

"Is it a skunk?" the lady asked.

"No," Hannah said. "Javelina. They're all over these parts."

"What's that?"

"Ugly, flea-bitten pigs," Pecos answered.

"Smell a bit like a skunk, though," Goldy added. "Kinda cute, sorta."

Naturally, Pete had to add his two cents on the matter. "You'll probably see some rooting around this evening. Don't get too close, though. They're usually not dangerous, but they are wild animals."

She knelt on the ground beside them uninvited. "What are you playing, cribbage?"

"Poker," Buddy answered. "Five-card draw, nothin' wild. Winner keeps the deal."

Lady Good-For-Nothing nodded and asked if she

could join in. She said she had played some poker before, her late husband had taught her, and would love to play now, not that she was any good, and if it was no intrusion. Pete rose. "Take my place," he said. "I think I'm going to turn in."

What chivalry, Hannah said to herself, as Pete left for his bedroll. The good lady took her place next to Hannah. She smelled like roses, and Hannah preferred the musky odor of the javelina. Hannah's mood didn't improve when she lost the next hand, holding two pair, kings over jacks, to Lady Gorgeous's three tens. Reluctantly, Hannah passed the deck to the English-woman, who shuffled the cards with perfection and said, "Gentlemen . . . and you, too Miss Scott, would you mind if we change the game to the one my late husband taught me?"

"Go right ahead," Pecos said.

"Our pleasure," Goldman said.

Lady Greedy began dealing without waiting for Hannah's reply. "Five-card draw," she said in her stupid accent, "jacks or better, trips to win."

Breaking a mustang and getting dusted more times than he cared to count . . . being embarrassed shooting glass targets . . . then herding a bunch of idiots around and traveling a short distance when they should have covered four times as many miles. Yeah, it had been a long, miserable day, and it was high time Pete Belissari turned in.

He reached down and grabbed the end of his gun-belt and started to unbuckle it, then looked at the butt of the revolver in the holster low on his hip. Pete glanced over his shoulder. No one was looking. Still, just to be safe, he stepped farther into the shadows, took a deep breath, and jerked the Colt from its holster. It came up quicker this time, but he fumbled trying to pull back the hammer. He dropped the revolver in the holster, and made another attempt. This time, the holster rode up on his hip, catching the barrel of the Colt. The revolver twisted and fell to the ground. Pete cringed, but luckily he hadn't cocked the weapon so it didn't accidentally discharge and blow off his foot.

Sighing, Belissari scooped up the Colt, unbuckled the belt and slammed the revolver into the holster. He placed the gunbelt and holster beside his bedroll, and knelt down, thinking about pulling off his moccasins but deciding against it, and fell onto the sugans, exhausted. He closed his eyes, thinking of the waves crashing back home in Corpus Christi, the smell of shrimp and saltwater, the hustle of the city, the feel of the salt spray. Sometimes he wondered. He was Greek, so why wasn't sailing the Gulf of Mexico with his father? Or why hadn't he attempted to please his mother and become a lawyer? He hoped he would dream tonight of red eggs, *tsouréki* bread, *mayerísta* soup and roasted lamb.

"Wake up, Peter! Wake up, lad!"

He pried his eyelids open, saw the hammy face of the honorable L. Merryweather Handal with a giant frown. Pete saw the darkening sky, realized he hadn't been asleep more than ten minutes. The hack writer pointed the Colt at Pete's throat. That sent any sleepiness out of Belissari's body in an instant. His right hand shot up and gripped the Colt's barrel.

"Handal," Pete cried out, and added a few Greek curses, pushing the barrel away. "Don't point that thing at me!"

The general ignored him, but allowed Pete to take the revolver. "You are The Greek Gun, Peter. Don't forget that, boy. And a gunman always sleeps with his deadly revolver, his friend and comforter. Your fingers should be gripped around the ivory handle of this equalizer, ready at the instant to leap up and ready to deliver wicked, everlasting death."

Sitting up, Belissari pointed the walnut-handled Colt at the empty holster. "I keep it handy, Colonel, but I'm not using it for a pillow."

"It's General Handal, if you please, sir. And you keep forgetting who is paying you the grand sum of one hundred and fifty dollars a month. Now, sir, do you sleep with the revolver, or do you force me to fire you and send you walking back to Fort Davis?"

Belissari sighed. *Walking*? He had brought his own horse, a blue roan gelding named Jason since he wanted to give Poseidon time to heal from his rodeo injuries (which is more than Pete had done for himself). But he relented, nodding his head wearily, and dropping back down, holding the Colt in his right hand, listening as Handal began humming *Oh, Dem Golden Slippers* and went back to entertain his guests.

His eyes closed. He felt the heavy revolver in his grip.

His eyes opened. He focused on the loaded Colt.

Sighing, he shut his eyes.

Sighing, he opened his eyes.

Belissari lifted his arm, resting his elbow on the hard ground, Colt in hand. Keeping his finger out of the trigger guard, he thumbed open the chamber gate and pulled the hammer to half-cock. Next he rotated the cylinder until five brass cartridges dropped to the ground. Satisfied, the Colt now unloaded, he snapped the chamber gate shut, slipped his finger against the trigger, pulled the hammer back to full-cock and lowered it. His arm and gun crashed to the ground. And, just in case Merryweather Handal came snooping around, Belissari covered the ejected shells with his battered hat.

Feeling safe, Pete closed his eyes and slept.

"Be extremely quiet," the honorable Brigadier General L. Merryweather Handal, esquire, whispered as he tiptoed around Pete Belissari's bedroll. "He looks sound asleep," he told Baron Van Hallstedt, Colonel Gustave Klint, Ludwig Schnitzler, and Carl Klint. "But at the slightest noise, The Greek Gun will jump up, ready for anything. See . . . see how he holds that lethal weapon at the ready. It's the mark of a brave gunman, a professional. Now come . . . but quietly . . . and we'll sample some peach brandy before calling it a night."

Petros Belissari, The Greek Gun, fearless man-killer and breaker of wild horses, rough-hewn hero of half-dime novels and graduate of the University of Louisville, friend of all other honest Texas frontiersmen and protector of the fair, weak, and underprivileged, continued to snore.

Chapter Seven

Pete Belissari would have patted himself on his back, only that would have hurt too much. Still, he had to be pleased. Baron Van Hallstedt loved his choice for a base camp, and so did the Klints, Herr Schnitzler, the Handals, and Lady Guinevere. Not that they had enjoyed the effort it took to get those cumbersome wagons up the mountains, but now that the three-day (not two) ordeal had ended, everyone seemed satisfied, downright happy.

They (*they* being Pete, Buddy, Nehemiah, Goldy and Rockwall) pitched tents in a clearing only a short hike to a beautiful pool of deep, cool water, complete with a small waterfall and cave deep enough for exploring but not deep enough where someone could get lost. Hannah pointed out the century plants to Handal's guests, explaining how the stalk shot out of the

57

agave only once during the plant's lifetime. The stalk grew to ten or even fourteen feet high over a period of many years, some say a hundred while others put it more like a decade, its yellow flowers blooming in the summer months, and then the century plant died.

Pete, however, was more concerned about the prospects of finding a wild mustang in these mountains than admiring cacti. At first light, he would take the baron on a scout farther up the mountains. They would build a corral trap in a watering hole in a box canyon—if he saw the signs—and wait. Meanwhile, Buddy Pecos would take Carl and Gustave Klint and Ludwig Schnitzler hunting along the lower elevations, leaving Hannah to look after the hired help, Handals, Eugene, and—Belissari grinned—Lady Guinevere.

Thoughts of those two stuck together for even just one day widened Pete's smile as he walked to the pool to fill canteens. He had just rounded the corner when he saw Lady Guinevere sunbathing on a rocky overhang above the deep water. She wore her red hair down and a polka-dot bathing suit that showed off a lot of arm and a good bit of calf. Belissari couldn't help but stare for a few seconds before he cleared his throat, not wanting to startle the good woman.

Which is exactly what he did.

She sat up suddenly, let out a terrified shriek, tried to stand, slipped on the wet granite and fell headfirst into the emerald water. Higher up on the rocks, to the right of Pete, he glimpsed a blur of movement. Mountain lion, he thought, but quickly realized it wasn't some animal, but a human: a miserable, spying little

Turk who must have thought Lady Guinevere had spotted him and was running for the nearest thicket.

Only he didn't make it either. He tripped and fell sideways into the pool.

It took only a second for Pete to react. He shunned his hat, gunbelt, the canteens and that stupid buckskin jacket and ran. Lady Guinevere's head appeared, then her arms, slapping the water around her violently. She spit out water and sank again. Belissari dived forward, aware of the Turk's screams for help. He reached the Englishwoman just as she broke the surface again, and Pete put his arm around her waist and tried to keep her above the water.

"Easy!" he told her, and she seemed to relax. Calm. That surprised him, for most people close to drowning would come close to pushing their would-be savior all the way to the center of the earth.

He saw a boulder nearby and with a firm grip on Lady Guinevere, kicked himself off the rocky wall toward it. Again, the woman remained relaxed and they reached the perch without incident. Pete helped her up. Sopping wet, she still looked so beautiful, and the way that bathing suit clung to her body almost made Belissari blush. She smiled at him and mouthed a silent, "Thank you."

"Wait here," he told her and swam toward the drowning Turk.

The first thing the Ottoman muck did was punch Pete in the jaw. He tried to gouge out Pete's eyes. He clawed his ear, pulled his long hair, slapped his nose, ripped his shirt, kicked him in the stomach, thigh, and chest. Finally, the wagon driver managed to put both hands on top of Pete's head and push him under, next tried to use Belissari's shoulders as a ladder or foot-rest. The toe of the Ottoman's boot cut a gash just below his left eye. Another heel hit him hard and he sank to the bottom. His brain screamed for oxygen. His lungs wanted to burst. Pete kicked up and broke free near the frothy waters the Turk kept churning. Belissari filled his lungs. He tried to tell the crazy numskull to calm down. The wagon driver pushed him under again.

Pete splashed through, spit out a mouthful of water, heard the commotion behind him, trying to find his bearings. He realized his position too late—his back faced the drowning man—and the Turk grabbed his shoulders, submerging Belissari once more. He strug-gled like a catfish on a trotline. A knee found his stom-ach. Pete groaned, choking on the water. Somehow, he managed to free himself, to push through the sur-face and cough, gag, and breathe. Eyes wide, the wagon driver screamed something in his abysmal lan-guage, and Pete drew back and slammed a right into the runt's hard head. He hit the Turk again, and the wretch relaxed.

Gripping the unconscious wagon driver around his chest, keeping the Turk's head above water, Pete swam the few yards until his moccasins touched the bed of the pool. He let go of the fool and sank to his knees, coughing out the water he had swallowed. As Belissari threw up, he heard the shouts from Ramón:

"Hurry! *Señor* Petros! He tries to kill Turk!"

He didn't really comprehend the words until, water, dinner, and breakfast purged from his stomach, he turned and grabbed the Turk's collar to drag him to shore. That's when the lariat looped over his chest and jerked him off his feet.

"Oh, I am certain Peter wasn't trying to kill that poor wagon driver," Lady Guinevere, her shoulders and bathing suit now covered with a woolen blanket, said in a soothing voice. "I mean, he saved me from a certain death, saved my poor Eugene from becoming an orphan."

Tom Rockwall shook his head, lariat still in his hands, and said: "Yeah, well Ramón says it looked like he was trying to drown him, and that's what it looked like to me, too, when I roped him."

"He hit me!" the Turk cried out. "He tried to murder me. Look at my face."

Belissari had heard enough. "Look at my face," he shot back, pointing to the cut and bruises. "Look at my shirt!" He hated to lose that, a good bib-front shirt made of red cotton that cost him ten bits. "You were drowning, and you came that close to drowning me."

Merryweather Handal cleared his throat. "Don't worry, ladies and gentlemen. We will get to the bottom of this."

Pete answered that with an oath. "We're not getting to the bottom of anything, Handal. I'm not going to be part of some mock trial. Turk here was spying on Lady Guinevere—"

"I was not," the driver blurted out. "Was gathering firewood."

Belissari didn't stop. "I came to fill the canteens. Lady Guinevere slipped. Turk ran. Both of them fell into the water. I saved the lady's life, then went to help the Turk, only he almost drowned me in the process. And use your heads, you dumb oafs. If I wanted to kill the son of a gun, I would have let him drown. He didn't need any help from me."

He stormed away from the would-be court-martial board and stomped soggily away to his bedroll and warbag. Pulling off his ruined shirt, mumbling a few choice curses in Greek and English, he grabbed his only extra shirt and some dry socks before marching into the trees to disrobe. Quit, he told himself. Head back to the Wild Rose Ranch. One hundred and fifty dollars? It wasn't worth it. But he knew he would stay.

"Petros?"

Belissari looked up, saw Hannah moving behind an alligator juniper.

"What?" he snapped, still irritable.

"I brought you a blanket. Give me your wet clothes and I'll put them by the fire."

He looked at the socks and shirt he had brought with him, wondered what good they would do when his moccasins, britches, and muslin underwear were soaked. "All right," he said, and finished stripping. He rolled his wet clothes into a ball and tossed them over the tree. They landed with a splat. Hannah giggled.

"The blanket?" he requested.

"Make me," she said. Giddy. It had been a long time since he had seen, or rather heard, Hannah this way.

Belissari stopped an oath before it got him in trouble and spoiled Hannah's humorous mood. He sighed, shook his head, and suddenly laughed at himself. The whole thing looked so silly. Lady Guinevere and Turk taking an unscheduled bath . . . Pete's fight to save the stupid sludge-head from drowning . . . being lassoed by Tom Rockwall . . . practically accused of attempted murder . . . his feral monologue . . . and now standing here, buck naked, wet, cold and, until now, humorless. "Pretty please," he begged.

"Suit yourself," she said and tossed the gray blanket onto a branch. He heard her pick up his clothes and head back to camp.

After drying off with the blanket, Pete wrapped it around himself and picked a way back to camp. He cut his right heel on a sharp rock and wound up hopping to the fire Hannah had going. Sitting down on the ground, he shook his head at his misery. Hannah came over and looked at his bleeding foot, spitting on it to clean the dirt and remarking, "You'll live." Buddy Pecos brought him a cup of coffee, and Dave Goldman added another log to the fire.

By the time Belissari was halfway finished with his second cup of coffee, the honorable Brig. Gen. L. Merryweather Handal moseyed over, brown jug in hand, and declared: "Peter, my good man, you'll be happy to know that I have exonerated you of all charges, and you are welcome to continue in our glorious expedition to seek out mustangs, wild game and other adventures that can only be found in this glorious vastness that is the wonderful frontier, raw yet beautiful, of the great state of Texas. Tomorrow, my dear scout, we shall go off chasing the wily steed, the twenty-hand black mustang known as El Lobo, unconquered, unbridled, unchained, unmistakable."

"We?" Pete asked.

"Certainly, Peter. I'm accompanying you and Baron Van Hallstedt. While Buddy here will take the rather wealthy Klints and Mr. Schnitzler hunting with my lovely wife, Jones."

"Jones?" Pecos asked.

"But, of course. My wife is a crack shot as you well know. That leaves Mr. Butterworth to protect Lady Guinevere, her darling boy, and Mrs. Klint from rough vermin like the ungodly Shoshone and Plomo's bandit gang."

"Plomo's dead, chief," Pecos said, "and we're a bit far south for Shoshone."

"Whatever." Handal took a pull and turned. "Sleep well, gents. Tomorrow will be another exciting day."

They ate supper by the fire after Hannah had served the rich guests and the Handals. Hannah remained in a good mood, picking at her beans and watching the stars. Buddy Pecos passed out cigars to Pete and Goldman. The three men lit up. After a few minutes, Belissari had forgotten about his miserable day.

"Think it'll rain?" Pecos asked.

"Nope," Goldman answered.

Hannah said: "Nice night," and Pete commented, "It certainly is. Perfect for a moonlight stroll."

"I'd like that," Hannah said softly.

Bliss, Pete thought. His cheek no longer throbbed, and his foot no longer bled. The fire warmed him, and he smiled thinking of Handal's vision of a wild black mustang named El Lobo. Now, he might be able to find a black mustang, but twenty hands high? That was an impossible order, a good five hands taller than any mustang he had ever caught.

"What are you smilin' 'bout?" Pecos asked.

Pete looked up, thinking the sharpshooter had addressed him, but saw Buddy staring at Goldy.

"Nothing much," Goldman said. "I was just thinking about how lucky I am. While Pete's out hunting dumb animals with that blowhard Baron and General Handal, and you're out with them other dudes trying not to get outshot by Mrs. Jones, well, I'll be back here just relaxing, in pretty close proximity to some might nice-looking females. Don't tell me y'all ain't noticed Miss Bonaventura. And Pete, gosh, you must have gotten an eyeful of Lady Guinevere this afternoon."

Now Pete Belissari liked David Goldman, was proud to call him a friend, but there were times when he could have shot the Missourian.

Hannah sat up ramrod straight and marched away in a huff.

"Want to go on that walk now?" Pete called out anxiously. She answered with silence.

Chapter Eight

Leaving their horses hobbled by a bubbling creek, Pete, Baron Van Hallstedt, and General Handal waded across the water and picked their way over boulders and through brush until they found a natural amphitheater set in the wall of a cliff. Pete's moccasin kicked around the gray-black dirt for a few seconds while Handal and the baron caught their breath. He knelt, picked up the artifact, and handed it to the Prussian visitor.

"Spear point," Belissari told the man who held the stone as if it might bite him.

"From what tribe?" Van Hallstedt asked.

Belissari shrugged. "Not sure. But they were probably here a thousand years before the Apache."

That didn't impress the Franco-Prussian War hero, and he tossed the relic to the ground. "So, why do you

66

bring me to this miserable place? No mustangs here, no?"

He pointed to the fading red drawings on the wall. "Indian drawings," he said. "Thought you might find these interesting. Very few have ever seen these before."

Handal moved excitedly to the wall. "Magnificent," he said, tracing his fingers along the small paintings of what appeared to be stick figures, animals and strange drawings.

"*Ach!*" said the Prussian, not interested, as he sat on a rock and rubbed his lower back.

"By jingo," Handal said, "for the first time in my life I have discovered a penmanship worse than mine."

Even Belissari had to laugh at that.

"What does it say?"

"You'd have to ask the men and women who wrote it," Pete answered, "and they've been gone for a mighty long time."

L. Merryweather Handal thought of this for a while. "Who knows?" he said at last. "The savage who wrote this billions of years ago back in the dark ages before Jesus Christ, Julius Caesar, and Cain and Abraham, why he could have been the great writer of his tribe, a troubadour and documenter of history, a storyteller, the best of his people. And now, all these years later, who should discover his prose but me, L. Merryweather Handal, arguably the best writer of the nineteenth century."

"Arguably," Pete agreed, trying not to grin. "Let's get back to the horses, see if we can find Baron Van Hallstedt his mustangs."

"*Ach!*" the European said again. "I should have brought Bonaventura with me. My boots. They are so dirty, caked with this filth. And no one to clean them."

Belissari shook his head. "Don't fret over them, Baron," he said. "They'll get a lot dirtier before we're through."

Hannah often wondered why she didn't ride up these mountains more often. They were beautiful in the summer, especially verdant this year with after all of the rains, a wonderful transition after the bitter droughts of years past. She heard the distant rumble of thunder and thought they might get a shower later this afternoon. The mountains always seemed peaceful, the perfect place to relax.

Not that she was relaxing now as she prepared vinegar pie. It was an easy recipe—sugar, flour, water, vinegar, butter, and four eggs—but not one of her favorites. Pete, ever a picky eater, hated it, said nobody would eat something called vinegar pie, to which she had snickered and mentioned the Greek dishes he sometimes concocted: *Féta* cheese smelled like a nasty goat, *glikó* coffee would never be mistaken for Arbuckles, and *avegolémono* soup was downright nasty. But Pete wasn't here, and the hired hands and Bonaventura didn't complain.

Of course, Lady Goober, her son, and the Klints wouldn't get vinegar pie. Nope, they were served, at their request, caviar, grilled rabbit, a nasty port wine, and stewed potatoes. Mr. Butterworth, acting as Merryweather Handal's emissary, joined them, and now he had taken Carl Klint out target shooting. The Klints had decided against going hunting today with Buddy and Dr. Schnitzler.

Hannah put the pie in a Dutch oven, covered the heavy lid with hot coals, and walked away. David Goldman couldn't be seen, so she approached Tom Rockwall instead. Of all the hired hands, she liked the big black man the best. He leaned against a wagon wheel, smoking a corncob pipe and reading a thick book that at first she thought must have been a bible.

Rockwall looked up, removed his pipe and tapped it on a small rock. "Evening," he said.

"Mr. Rockwall. Supper should be ready in an hour."

He closed the book.

"I didn't mean to intrude," she said. "Go back to your reading."

"You are no intrusion, Miss Hannah. Have a seat." He gestured toward the ground.

She knelt, trying to think of something to say. "What are you reading?"

Rockwall returned the pipe stem to his mouth and sucked hard. Tapping on the leather cover, he replied after exhaling. "A history of the war against the Zulu."

"That must be interesting."

"All history is interesting, Miss Hannah. And important."

She laughed at that. "I wish I could make my orphans think that. All but two of them hate to read anything, especially history. And the two that do read, one only wants to stick his nose in a five-penny dreadful, and the other loves only Jane Austen."

Tom Rockwall shrugged his broad shoulders. "I'm sure we were the same way when we were young, making teaching as hard as possible for our educators."

"Likely." She thought back to the Travis County Orphanage and bone-headed, pointy-nosed, spiteful old Mr. Monieth trying to teach arithmetic. "Now, young waifs," he had said in his awful monotone, "if Stanson Rogers has fourteen apples and takes seven more from Fred Patten—" Eight-year-old Fred had yelled: "Stanson'll have a black eye if he takes any of my apples."

Hannah looked up as Rockwall continued. "I guess one must have a knack for history, and I'll admit I have no knack for Jane Austen. But through history we learn from our past, learn not to make the same mistakes over and over. It's important."

The trees began to rustle in the wind, and thunder rolled. The skies darkened. She might have to set up a cover over her cook fire if it started raining. But she had a while.

"You sound like you should be a schoolteacher, Mr. Rockwall."

He smiled. "College actually, Miss Hannah. I attended, graduated from, and then taught at the American Missionary Society College in Atlanta, Georgia."

And now he was driving a wagon in West Texas. She considered this, but said nothing. You didn't ask someone why he came west. You didn't even ask a man his name in this part of the country. Instead, she said, "Perhaps I can interest you into addressing my terrors when we're finished here, give them a history lesson."

"I'd be delighted, Miss Hannah."

She laughed again. "Maybe you can even teach them math."

The black man shook his head. "Alas, I never had the knack with numbers, at least not to teach school-age children."

"Math never was my strongest subject either."

They fell silent. Eugene began to whine in his tent about the approaching thunder. Hannah looked around to study the clouds. They didn't look like some frog-strangler or serious electrical storm. And they were safe here from the hazards of a flash flood. No, this would be a gentle rain. Little Eugene had nothing to fear.

That's what Lady Granite-Heart told him, first kindly, then harshly. The boy whined. The slap carried across the camp, followed by the perfect lady's not-so-refined voice, "Shut your bloody trap!" The boy whined no more.

Hannah and Rockwall exchanged glances but said nothing. She felt the first drops of rain, and rose, her knees cracking, to return to the fire. Tom Rockwall slid his book into a canvas bag and also stood, drawing on the pipe stem. As Hannah turned to leave, he said, "I'll give you a math lesson, Miss Hannah."

She waited.

"The Battle of Ntombe Drift was fought in March of '79."

He said nothing else, gave no explanation, just turned and left. Hannah's eyes followed him as he tossed his book bag into the back of a wagon and went to check on the horse herd with Ramón.

What on earth was he talking about? she asked herself.

To put it mildly, Baron Van Hallstedt did not take kindly to making camp in a small, damp cave to escape the rain. He threw himself into a royal fit, barking out harsh words that needed no interpreter. Why had not Belissari and Handal brought a pack animal with them full of tents, good food, and dry clothes? he bellowed. Because, Pete explained, he liked to travel light when chasing mustangs—and the wagons and chow weren't that far away if the uppity baron wanted to leave.

Pete was staying.

He had found the horse apples early in the afternoon, and felt his heart beating the way it used to, felt the blood rushing through his veins, the anticipation of finding and capturing a herd of wild horses. From the signs, this herd looked to be small, maybe a stallion and six or seven mares, but he liked that. The big herds had been driven out of this country, and one man—he couldn't count on the baron or Handal—wouldn't be able to handle too many. He hadn't been hunting mustangs in years, and chasing, capturing, and breaking a wild herd of horses was a job that suited him much better than guiding around a bunch of snobs and a Turkish weasel. He'd gladly forfeit the one-fifty General L. Merryweather Handal had promised.

But the baron calmed down a bit after Handal liberally spiked his coffee with peach brandy. The Prussian muttered throughout the meal that Pete's coffee was too strong, the salt pork too greasy, and the American's appetite for cold biscuits seemed quite silly.

"Wet, cold . . . this is disgusting," Van Hallstedt said. "When shall we be finished with this mustanging?"

Belissari told him it could be a week or a month or six months. Handal gave the war hero a cigar to pacify him. War hero? How could a war hero be bothered by a little rain and some mud? Granted, the conflict between France and Prussia had been over fifteen–sixteen years, and maybe the good baron had become too used to being waited on hand and foot by Bonaventura and other servants, but . . .

"How do you do this mustanging?" the baron asked suddenly, placated at last by the small fire, cheap cigar, and Merryweather Handal's brandy.

"There are different methods," Pete explained. "Some mustangers just like to ride down to the herd and give chase—"

"Capital!" Handal exclaimed. "We shall ride down those poor beasts, giving chase, a relentless pursuit with the only sound being the wind in our faces and the sharp pounding of our horses' shod feet."

"Well," Pete said. "Usually, the mustangers have extra horses when they try it that way. And that can take a long time. The stallion will run as long as he can, trying to lose the pursuers. It's hard riding all day, all night, as long as it takes. Can be dangerous."

L. Merryweather Handal belched. "Dangerous is my middle name, sir. But perhaps we should take our trusty steeds into account. Yes, out here a man is only as good as his mount, and since you lacked the foresight to bring extra horses on this jaunt, we shall be forced to capture those wily beasts another way."

Pete nodded. "I met one man some years back by the name of Bob Lemmons, and he told me the key to capturing a *manada* was to become a mustang, live like one." He shook his head in admiration. "And I believe he probably did, likely ate grass and slept standing up. He'd find sign and just follow the tracks, catch up and stay with the herd until the stallion and mares accepted him. After a while, once the animals trusted him, he'd take them to water, and afterward it would be easy. Always wish I could do it his way."

"Rubbish," the baron said. "A fanciful story."

"You never smelled Bob Lemmons after he brought in a *manada*, Baron. Anyway, the way I usually do it, since I work alone and don't quite have the mind of a mustang, is to find a water hole and build a corral trap around it. Once the herd comes in, I close the gate."

"Sounds dull," Van Hallstedt commented.

Belissari shrugged. "Breaking those horses is enough excitement for me."

The baron pitched the stub of his cigar into the fire. "Do not some of you mustangers shoot the stallion?"

"Sometimes, a stallion will be so wild, relentless he'll kill himself, or maybe a mustanger will shoot him—I never have."

"No. I mean to crease the animal with a bullet, stun him, so that you can capture him."

"You'd have to be a mighty good shot to get away with that one, Baron."

Chapter Nine

Lady Her-Graciousness turned up her nose and tightened her lips. Her eyes began watering, and she finally dared to open her mouth to ask Hannah: "Is that smell a javelina?"

"No," she answered. "It's Buddy Pecos."

The tall sharpshooter stood at the edge of camp, per Hannah's orders after he first arrived back from a none-too-successful hunting expedition. Of course, Hannah had smelled the Texan long before she saw him. "I got skunked," he explained sheepishly, and Hannah tried hard not to laugh at his misfortune. She sent him to the edge of camp, which seemed like a good idea until the wind changed directions. Now as the others returned to camp from target practice, afternoon strolls, or a swim in the pool, they began taking exception to the foul odor.

"What are you going to do about it, Miss Scott?" Lady Gag-a-lot asked.

"Working on it."

Guinevere promptly, stiffly, retired to her tent and closed the canvas flap. Hannah finished heating up a mixture of canned tomatoes and water, then struggled to carry the heavy pot toward Buddy. No one offered to help, not even the polite Nehemiah and Rockwall or friendly Dave Goldman. Of course, Hannah couldn't blame anyone for wanting to keep their distance from the hunting guide right now. She held her breath as long as she could before gasping and setting the pot on a rock while Buddy Pecos stood smoking a cigarette.

"What's that?" he asked.

"Tomatoes and water," she said. "I want you to bathe in this, just use a rag and wipe it over your entire body. And get rid of your clothes. We'll burn those."

"You expect me to run 'round naked with all them jaybirds?" he said.

"Trust me, Buddy. No one's going to be spying on you for quite a while. Take this pot to the pool, and don't come back till you're presentable. I'll find your clothes and bring them near."

Pecos crushed out his cigarette with a boot heel. "I ain't got no spare duds, Hannah. That's what I been tryin' to tell you."

Hannah paused. Having never been skunked before, and never having one or her orphans or friends on the receiving end of the animal, Hannah wasn't exactly certain how well her remedy would work. She didn't have to rid the smell completely. After all, after a few days out here, pretty soon everyone would be a tad sour, even the perfect English tart.

"You didn't bring anything? Not even another shirt?"

"Nope."

"But what happens if you get wet?"

"Then I'm wet. And if a sleeve gets ripped off by mesquite, then I'm sleeveless. And if I get skunked, well, I smell."

She pursed her lips. Buddy smelled a little bit, and sometimes a lot, even when he wasn't skunked. Right now, he could make dirty Jones Handal smell like rose blossoms. "All right," she said, rebounding, "then wash your clothes in the pot after you've bathed in my concoction. Now, did you kill the skunk?"

"No, ma'am. I just stepped through some *piñon* without lookin' where I was goin', like some dumb greenhorn, and the next thing I knowed, I was gettin' sprayed and that she-skunk was a-lightin' a shuck for parts unknown."

Pity, Hannah thought. Skunk grease was a pretty good treatment for croup. She ordered Buddy to stay at the pool tonight. She'd bring him his bedroll and some supper later. Pecos picked up the pot and nonchalantly made his way through the trees and rocks toward the water. She glanced skyward. It looked like rain, another afternoon thunderstorm. Good. That might wash away some of the rankness. Suddenly, she laughed. Pete was lucky, as usual. He was off doing what he loved, mustanging, and didn't have to put up with such stupidity and constant complaining.

Hannah filled her lungs with fresh, non-polluted air,

and walked back to camp. She had supper to fix. The
Klinks had requested stewed cabbage. That would
work, Hannah reasoned. About the only thing she
could think of that smelled worse than skunk was
cooked cabbage.

Baron Van Hallstedt sat fanning himself in the
shade, passing the brown clay jug every once in a
while to Brig. Gen. L. Merryweather Handal. The afternoon sun scorched everything in its path, including
one Petros Belissari. Stripped to his waist, panting,
Pete wiped the sweat from his brow and stared at the
two men and thought, again, that his reasoning for
taking this job wasn't so sound after all.

Yesterday afternoon, after Pete told Handal and the
baron to tie their horses up, Van Hallstedt secured his
mount to a mere sapling. The horse was greener than
a juniper grove, and at the first roll of thunder, it up-
rooted the tree and started loping around the camp,
pulling the tree behind it.

Now to a horse, that small tree looked like a giant
monster, so it squealed, eyes wide, and raced on and
on and on. The good baron laughed, but Pete knew it
wouldn't be funny if the horse injured, possibly killed,
itself and set the Franco-Prussian War hero afoot. Not
in this country. Of course, Pete was well aware that
General Handal would demand that Pete relinquish Jason to the paying guest. Anyway, to make a long story
short, Belissari caught the panicked animal at last, dis-
engaged the tree, and, once the horse had calmed
down, tethered the animal properly.

Yet for all his complaints, Belissari still felt excited.

He found a water hole with plenty of mustang sign, so now all he had to do was build a corral to catch the herd when they came in to water. He had built pens such as this one before by himself. Yet he thought maybe, just maybe, Handal and the baron would offer some assistance.

Yeah, that was going to happen. Just look at the sloths. He should have scouted his old stamping grounds. With luck he could have found another herd watering at one of the holes where he had already built a pen. Then all he would have to do would be repair the corral, rather than build a new one. But with the mustangs so rare here, the chances of that seemed about as good as . . . well, getting Van Hallstedt and Merryweather Handal off their lazy behinds.

He slid another sturdy post into a hole, making sure it would hold firm before continuing. When finished, the corral would be big, enclosing the water hole, and circular. Good mustangers knew better than to build a corral with corners because a stallion, and sometimes the mares, would slam into the corner walls over and over again until they busted out or died trying.

Once he had the corral's perimeter built, he would cut branches off trees and gather shrubs and pile them at the corral's one gate, making a narrow pathway— "the green line," old-time mustangers called it—that the wild horses would follow. For some reason, they would avoid touching the "green line," even though the makeshift fence couldn't hold a jackrabbit. The mustangs would run straight into the corral to the water hole. Maybe Pete, Handal, and the baron would chase the herd, shouting, yelling, waving their arms.

Once the last mare went through "the green line" and was inside the corral, Pete would bar the gate, and that would be that.

Then the fun began. Roping the horses. Fastening a rope around a mustang's neck and the fetlock joint of a front leg to keep the animal from escaping. A few days later, Pete would begin gentling the mustangs, getting them used to saddle and bridle. Some mustangers kept food and water from the captives for almost a week, but Pete never could see the reason behind that. Two days. Maybe three. That seemed long enough. He wanted to tame the horses, not break their spirit. He wanted the animals to learn to trust him, not fear him. The hardest to tame would be the stallion. Once he submitted, the mares, generally, would readily follow.

His back and arms ached, and his shoulders felt raw from the sun, when he finally finished the corral. After drenching his knotted, sweaty hair in the water, he gathered up his tools and clothes and approached his two companions.

"Done?" Van Hallstedt asked.

Pete felt too tired to answer verbally. A nod would have to suffice.

L. Merryweather Handal clapped his hands. "Now what, my friend?"

Belissari reached for the brown jug. The baron frowned but offered no resistance when Pete raised it and took a long pull of . . . corn whiskey? Handal must be out of brandy. The liquor burned his throat, but felt soothing. Then again, as tired as he was, coal oil would probably have tasted just as fine.

"We wait," he answered at last.

The sigh came from Van Hallstedt. Pete handed the jug back. "This mustanging, it tries one's patience, no?"

At that, Pete had to grin. "It tries one's patience, yes. But when it works, there's no better feeling."

They made camp in a nearby gully. Once they heard the mustangs, they would wait. Pete decided against chasing the horses through "the green line." Maybe if Handal and the baron had more experience, he would have risked it. He explained to the two men that once the animals galloped inside the corral, he would sneak up and bar the gate. Easy.

"Is this how all mustangers make their corrals?" the baron asked.

Belissari shook his head. "Sometimes, what I do is build a smaller corral, a catch pen. It's similar to this and the method is the same. Wait for the *manada* to come water, then bar the gate. Others make big, winding corrals—a *caracol*—with wings. And I've seen mustangers make corrals out of nothing more than a wagon cover. Since the horse can't see through it, he figures it's as solid as a mountain wall. And I've known a few men who like to stake out mares to lure the mustangs in."

The baron shook his head. "I don't see much sport in these methods."

"You'll get your share of sport once we try to break the horses."

"Yes," Handal said, "remember the rodeo in Pecos. Well, soon, my foreign friend, you'll have your own private rodeo."

Baron Van Hallstedt grunted and drained the corn whiskey.

He watched the black stallion in awe. Rearing, forelegs punching the air like a pugilist in training, kicking up clouds of dust in the gloaming. Belissari wet his lips and then bit them. The mustang was cautious, not trusting "the green line." Behind him waited his *manada*, ten mares. Sorrels, grullos, roans, and duns. A great catch, if only the black would cooperate.

It stopped rearing, but continued to toss its head, nostrils flaring, pawing the earth with its unshod hooves. Right now, Pete really didn't care if the stallion led his mares to water or went elsewhere. He simply enjoyed the spectacle of nature he was witnessing for the first time in years.

"By jingo . . . Peter . . . you've done it!" Handal said between pants after laboring up from camp.

"Quiet," Pete whispered. "Don't want to scare them off."

"Yes. Certainly. But I must admit, this is a wonderful glimpse of the raw West. By Jove, a scene like this could be on the cover of my next literary classic, don't you think?"

Not enough violence, Pete thought about saying, remembering those dreadful covers of tall, dashing heroes with guns and knives, surrounded by enemies with even more weapons, but he only nodded in polite agreement.

"Best run tell the baron," Belissari suggested. "He might enjoy this."

"Of course, of course," and Handal half-stumbled, half-trotted back to camp.

Pete felt a bit selfish, though, as he watched the wild horses. He wished he were alone, sharing this with no one.

Chapter Ten

Master Eugene celebrated his sixth birthday the following day, and Hannah, despite feeling strong contempt for the boy's mother, made it a grand occasion. She did her best to turn out a Dolly Varden cake in a Dutch oven, although she had to replace the currants the recipe called for with more raisins and had to find quail eggs to complete the dish. The cake didn't look anything like the masterpiece she had seen Charles Buehler create at his Fort Davis bakery, but the butter cream frosting hid most of the mistakes. She put one candle in the center of the cake, and everyone applauded when Eugene blew out the flame. *Blew out?* Well, actually the kid doused the wick with saliva.

"Make a wish," his mother said.

Idiot, Hannah muttered. You were supposed to make the wish before you blew out the candle.

No one complained about the grub. Dave Goldman tousled the boy's hair, wished him many happy birthdays in return, and walked away with a handful of cake, disappearing behind one of the wagons. Nonchalantly, too. Goldy never was nonchalant about anything. He was a Missouri hillbilly. A few minutes later, Bonaventura excused herself, wishing Eugene a happy birthday, and walked toward her wagon, only she took a detour when she thought no one was looking—and nobody was, except Hannah—and went in the same direction as David.

Hannah Scott collected the dirty dishes and smiled. She found herself reciting the old rhyme of the Travis County Orphanage:

Dave and Bonaventura sitting in a tree.

K-i-s-s-i-n-g.

Buddy Pecos, his skunky smell somewhat dissipated, handed Eugene a rabbit's foot, the only gift the boy received. Even his own mother had not given him a present. Hannah wished she had something for the child. Maybe when they got back to the ranch she could let him have some hand-me-down toy. What kind of mother was this Lady Guinevere? Not even a birthday present for her only son.

That thought soured Hannah's mood considerably as she scrubbed the dishes in the wreck pan. She mumbled a few unladylike phrases under her breath, and didn't smile again until David Goldman stood in front of her, offering to help.

"No thanks," she said. "I'm almost done."

She dried a plate with her apron. "How was your stroll?"

Goldy's face turned ashen. "Ma'am?"

"I saw you walk toward the pool."

"Oh." He glanced every which way before continuing. "Just felt like a walk. Thought I might try to scare up a deer or something for supper."

With a nod, Hannah picked up the last plate. "Most people take a rifle or shotgun with them when they go hunting, Dave," she said softly.

"Yeah. Well. Well, I wasn't thinking."

She dried the plate and set it on the chuckwagon. "I understand. I imagine a pretty girl like Bonaventura could make a man forget a lot of things."

Dave Goldman cleared his throat, shuffled his feet, and looked around nervously. "Miss Hannah, now please don't tell nobody about us. We're just getting to know each other. I mean them men she works for, the baron and Doc Ludwig, well, they'd raise Cain if they were to find out about us. They treat her like dirt." He swore softly. "They treat us all like dirt. Don't that rile you?"

With a shrug, Hannah answered, "I don't rightly care how they act, Dave. They'll be gone soon, out of our hair. What bothers me is how a mother can ignore her only son's birthday."

"Well, me, I thought we outlawed slavery in this country."

"It's not slavery, Dave. It's just a European class system. They're the upper class, the money, the royalty, and we're the servants, the peasants, the dirt."

"You ever been to Europe?"

She laughed. "Not any closer than Dickens or Dumas."

"Well, I don't think I'd like to go there. Not if all of them act this way. If you ask me, I think the only decent ones on this trip is us dirt-class types: me and you, Tom . . ."

Hannah added: ". . . and Bonaventura."

Dave smiled at last. "Yeah, especially her."

"I think you two make a nice couple."

"Thanks," he said. "Sure wish I could speak Italian, though."

She awoke before dawn, dressed, stumbled to the chuckwagon, and turned up the lantern. She had breakfast to fix. Flapjacks and sausage for the Klints, Lady Greatness, and Eugene, and bacon and warmed-over biscuits for the hired help. Buddy Pecos, Jones Handal, Ludwig Schnitzler, and Mr. Butterworth had already left, without eating, for another hunting trip.

Pecos planned to take the party after some antelope or deer. They'd be gone all day, maybe two. With luck, by the time they returned, they would have antelope steaks. After that, maybe Pecos would let the guests rest a couple of days and he'd scout out after Pete to see how the great horseman was faring with General Handal and Baron Van Hallstedt.

Hannah tried to figure out how to divide up the sausage for the guests. How many mouths did she have to feed this morning? How many pieces of smoked sausage to go around? More math. She recalled her conversation with Tom Rockwall when his words suddenly ran through her brain once more: *The Battle of Ntombe Drift was fought in March of '79.*

1879. Tom Rockwall had told her it was a math

equation, and now she understood. Eugene was six years old. His father, according to Lady Glorious, had been killed in that massacre. The math didn't work. No matter how you figured it, that boy had been born almost one and a half years after his alleged father died. So what did this mean? A child out of wedlock? Or maybe Lady Guinevere had told some cock-and-bull story to earn her pity. She found that theory more reasonable, if only for Eugene's sake. So the proper British witch was just a plain old liar. Hannah scoffed. Her detective work pleased her immensely. Miss Gutted-Fish was no lady. That was for certain.

She couldn't wait to tell Pete her findings. Not that he would give her any satisfying reaction. He'd probably shrug and grunt something unintelligible. No, he would inform her that out here, in the West, you didn't pry into other people's affairs. You minded your own business. Which she knew, of course, and usually practiced. But Lady Grotesque didn't deserve Western courtesy.

"Mommie! Mommie!" Eugene shouted. "Look at that elk!"

It wasn't an elk, but a deer. A doe on the edge of the camp. Hannah smiled at the boy's excitement, but the smile turned upside down when she realized the animal was wounded. It stood wobbly, blood dripping onto the ground from a bullet hole above the left shoulder. Buddy Pecos had taken a group hunting, and Hannah guessed this poor doe was one of the victims. Too bad somebody couldn't shoot better than that.

Eugene ran toward the doe. Hannah called out for

him to stop. Wild animals, especially wounded ones, were far from friendly. The boy didn't listen. Luckily, Bonaventura ran forward and caught the squealing kid while the doe, scared, bounded twice and fell on its side. Hannah saw the deer breathing heavily. She walked from the chuckwagon toward the dying animal.

The doe's eyes were beginning to glaze over. Hannah knelt over it, frowning. She enjoyed venison as much as anyone, but she hated to see any animal suffer. A shadow crossed her face. Ramón Armando stood above her. The *vaquero* looked mighty pale.

"She's been shot," Hannah told him. "We need to put her out of her misery."

The Mexican understood. He knew Hannah meant that *he* should kill the doe. Armando backed away, palms held upward, shaking his head. "No. Me no can kill. *Por favor.* You do it."

"Ramón," she pleaded. Then she knew what he meant. *She* didn't want to kill the doe, even though it was necessary.

Armando pulled a Barlow knife from the pocket on his chaps, tested the razor-sharp edge with a hair plucked from his head, and handed the knife to Hannah. When she took it, he made the sign of the cross and hurried away from the bloody scene. Hannah shook her head at the *vaquero*'s weak stomach.

Placing one hand over the doe's frantic eye, she bit her lip and deftly cut the animal's throat, backing away as the blood stained the ground. She wiped the bloody blade on her apron and heard Lady Ohmigosh blurt out an "Oh my gosh." Hannah suddenly remembered little Eugene.

"Oh my gosh," Hannah said, and slipped the Barlow knife into the pocket on her apron and spun around.

Here she was, preaching to herself about what a poor mother Lady Guinevere could be. Yet Hannah had just shown no consideration for a six-year-old kid who just moments before had been excited about seeing a wild deer so close to camp. Hannah groaned, and turned around to apologize to the boy.

He had freed himself from Bonaventura's grip and stood just a few feet from Hannah, staring at the bloody carcass. His mouth hung on its hinges, and his eyes were wide. He blinked, studied the dead doe once more. Next, his gaze fell upon Hannah.

"Hey, lady," he said, "stick that elk again with your knife. Make it bleed some more."

Goldman, Nehemiah, and Rockwall, who had missed the excitement because they were gathering firewood, returned just in time to inherit the dirty work of hoisting the doe up a tree to drain the blood and gut the animal. There would be venison steaks for supper, and Hannah made sure the three men cut thin strips of meat to dry in the sun for later.

Buddy Pecos returned with his hunting group empty-handed once again. At least, he thought they had come up empty until he spotted the deerskin pegged down in the sun.

"You mean that is the antelope I killed?" Carl Klint asked.

"Deer," Buddy corrected. "I mean that's the doe you wounded. Hannah here kilt it."

"*Danke*," he said, bowing graciously to Hannah.

Hannah shrugged.

"I must show everyone," he said, grinning, and practically ran to his parents' wagon.

Buddy Pecos sent a mouthful of tobacco juice sizzling in the fire. He shook his head and moved the plug of tobacco into the other cheek.

"Fed up?" Hannah asked.

"Plumb near."

"Not much hunters, are they?"

The Texan shook his head. "Aw, that Butterworth gent knows how to carry a gun. I suspect he's used that Colt of his a time or two on bigger game than deer. And the colonel's new wife, well, she may not be what we'd call a real lady back in East Texas, but she'd be one to ride the river with if you was bein' chased by Comanch or outlaws. She's about as good a shot as me." He spit again.

"I reckon them Klints and all is happy just to be out here in the middle of nowhere. They don't seem that interested in huntin', 'ceptin' young Carl. And Carl, well, he means well, but he just ain't got the knack when it comes to huntin'. And considerin' all the powder he's burned target shootin' with Butterworth, you'd think he'd be a mite better hand with a gun." He shook his head, his teeth working on the tobacco as if it were a leathery tough piece of steak. "And I can't complain about the money Handal's promisin' us. But I got to be honest with you, Hannah. These dandies can sure drive a body loco."

"Amen," Hannah mumbled under her breath.

"How's that?"

"Nothing."

Pecos shook his head. "We spotted that doe, and I told Carl where to shoot, told him not to jerk the trigger. Probably should have asked Mrs. Handal to cover him just in case and pop that critter if Klint missed. Anyway, he botched the job, and we spent the rest of the day trailin' the poor doe all the way back here. Sure hope we don't get jumped by Apaches."

"Not much chance of that," Hannah said.

Pecos stretched. "Well, I'd best clean Carl's rifle. I sure hope Pete's makin' out better trackin' mustangs than I am huntin'."

Hannah smiled. "I'm sure he is."

Chapter Eleven

By the time Merryweather Handal returned, the mustangs still had refused to enter "the green line."

"Where's the baron?" Pete asked.

"He's coming." The writer caught his breath. "Why don't they go in?"

Pete shrugged. "Mustangs don't stay free being careless. Give him time."

Handal smiled. "Ah, to watch this, my friend, I now know what The Bard meant when he wrote: 'Speak to the earth, and it shall teach thee.' "

Belissari smiled. The quotation came from the Book of Job, not William Shakespeare. But Pete was in too good a mood to correct the dime novelist.

The black stallion reared again, then turned toward the mares. He seemed to be calming down, ready to lead his herd to the water. Pete let out a slow breath.

The gunshot deafened him, and the muzzle blast singed his hair. With a yell, Belissari grabbed his ringing ear, trying to fight back the pain. Tears welled in his eyes, and he fell on all fours, knocking off his hat, and dropped to the ground, writhing. When he opened his eyes, he glimpsed a blur shooting past him. He seemed to know it was Baron Van Hallstedt, clumsily carrying a Remington Rolling Block rifle as he scurried toward the mustangs. Pete sat up, still holding his ear, blinking away tears until his vision cleared. He saw General L. Merryweather Handal's face masked in shock. The novelist asked, "Are you all right?" But Pete couldn't understand the words.

Belissari swore in Greek and English until the pain subsided and the ringing died down. Slowly he stood, sweeping up his battered hat, and took a couple of steps toward the corral he had built for nothing, thanks to the good baron. He saw the Franco-Prussian War hero stumbling ahead of them, shouting something in his native tongue.

The mustang mares were gone, scattered like dust in a West Texas windstorm. They wouldn't stop running until morning. The black stallion lay on its side, not moving.

"He must have tried that crease shot," Handal said, and now Pete could hear the words. "Maybe it worked. The horse isn't moving."

Pete spat out another curse. "That's because he's dead."

In all his years, Pete Belissari had never heard of anyone making a successful crease shot. It required close range, which the baron didn't have, and a steady patience and great deal of luck, both of which he also lacked. You generally aimed at a spot near the horse's withers, maybe twelve or fourteen inches below the ears. In theory, the bullet would barely nick the spinal nerve at the top of the mustang's neck, leaving the horse stunned, unable to move, for a few minutes. Just long enough to tie the mustang.

And that's all it was: theory. Anyone who said he creased mustangs successfully was a liar.

A couple of times, Pete had captured mustangs that had been lucky victims of some fool who had tried a crease shot. A bullet hole had scarred over the necks of the animals near their windpipes. Both times, Pete had been amazed the mustangs had survived the wounds. He named one of the horses Lucky and the other Scar Neck, and sold both mounts to the U.S. Army at Fort Davis. The stallion shot by Van Hallstedt hadn't been so fortunate.

The baron stood over the beautiful black beast and shook his head slowly. Pete and Handal stopped in front of the dead mustang. The .45–70 bullet had slammed into the stallion's head, not even close to the "crease target," killing it instantly.

"Pity," Van Hallstedt said. "The horse move at the last second. Next time I have more luck, no?"

He smiled and tossed the rifle to Pete. "Carry my rifle back, please. I'm tired."

Belissari caught the heavy rifle. He pictured himself raising the Remington and blowing the baron's head off, but the Rolling Block was a single shot, and Pete didn't have a shell. The baron glanced at the dead animal once more, saying "pity" again before stepping around the blood and walking between the horseman and Handal.

Next time? Pete Belissari seethed. His knuckles whitened as he clenched the Remington. There wouldn't be a next time. Those mares would never return to this watering hole, and it would be a long time before another group of mustangs would drink here. They'd smell the blood and the dead stallion long after the blood had soaked into the ground and wolves had scattered the horse's bones. Belissari thought about the corral he had built. He thought about the sweat, and the baron's laziness and arrogance. Pete's ears began to burn. He felt the blood boiling, racing to his brain. He glanced at the mustang and took two steps after the pompous baron.

"No!" L. Merryweather Handal shouted.

But Pete had already raised the rifle like a club over his head. He couldn't kill the baron, couldn't shoot down the fool in cold blood, although he deserved it. Belissari didn't think about the consequences, didn't think about the money Handal was paying. He didn't think about anything except the dead mustang.

Baron Van Hallstedt turned around just in time to see the Remington's downward arc. He froze, mouth open, and watched the heavy rifle come down . . . down . . . down . . . slowly, as if the world had stopped spinning. The baron's hat softened the blow, stopped his head from being split open. He crumpled to the ground with a groan, still conscious, eyes staring upward at the darkening sky.

"How does it feel?" Belissari yelled.

*   *   *

The homecoming at base camp went about as Pete had expected. Although, he had to admit, things could have been worse. General Handal talked the baron out of swearing out a complaint and having Belissari jailed in Fort Davis for assault and battery. Hannah sided with Pete, saying Van Hallstedt deserved everything he got, but she agreed that it would be best if Pete stayed behind at the ranch.

Not that he had any say in the matter. The Handals and Butterworth all agreed that Belissari had to be fired. They couldn't have guides go around clubbing their paying customers with a rifle that weighed more than nine pounds. Pete tried to remember the last time he had been fired—had he ever been fired?

Good riddance to the whole lot, he thought. He'd look after the kids, work on the ranch, get things back in order while Hannah sweated like a scullery maid for these ne'er-do-wells. They would break camp and head back to Fort Davis. From there, Gen. L. Merryweather Handal promised the Klints, Van Hallstedt, Dr. Schnitzler, Lady Guinevere, and Eugene a spectacular adventure into the rugged Big Bend country of the Chihuahuan Desert.

A few more days, and he'd be done with them, Pete thought as he took the nose bag off Jason. He patted the horse's neck, and turned around just in time to see the Turk and dodge the knife that slashed at Belissari's abdomen.

Pete jumped back as the blade passed again. He moved away from the horse, watching both the knife and the Turk's glare. "I kill you, you Greek—" Turk spat. "I gut you like a fish. You try to kill the baron. For that, I kill you."

Pete wet his lips, considering his odds. His assailant held the weapon easily, displaying the silver blade like some teenager showing off, not an accomplished knife fighter. Besides, Turk had only a knife. He didn't seem to comprehend that all Pete had to do was pull the revolver from his holster and send the little weasel to join his Ottoman ancestors.

Yet Belissari didn't need to resort to a gun. At least, not yet. He was stubborn enough, proud enough, to believe he could whip that runt, knife or not, without having to draw an equalizer. A Greek didn't need a handgun to defeat a Turkish louse.

With a sneer, Turk lunged. Belissari tossed the empty feed bag into Turk's face. The wagon driver stumbled and fell to his knees. Some fighter, Belissari muttered to himself, and kicked the idiot hard in the face. His moccasin foot caught Turk full, smashing his nose and lips. Pete hoped the blow knocked out a few teeth, too. Turk went sprawling one way and his knife the other. He landed on his back, behind Belissari's horse, and shook his head, slowly, trying to comprehend what had just happened. Pete tried not to gloat. Instead, he waited patiently. He saw Goldman, Rockwall, Ramón, and Handal running to stop the ruckus.

Of course, the fight was already over. Pete knew that. And unless the wagon driver was dumber than he looked, he also knew it.

As soon as Turk got on his feet, Jason kicked him. The iron hooves smacked the would-be knife fighter's buttocks. Serves him right, Pete thought, for starting a fight amid a bunch of green horses.

The little runt went sailing out of the makeshift corral. He landed on his back, his spindly legs kicking upward for a second, then stopped moving at all.

"Break it up!" Handal said, grasping Pete's arms, although Pete hadn't moved since kicking Turk in the face. Ramón and Tom Rockwall helped the bleeding Turk to his feet. The driver swore something in his abysmal language and pulled himself from his helpers.

"I need no one!" he yelled, and walked—no, limped—back to camp, gently rubbing his rear end with both hands.

Dave Goldman found the Turk's knife and rubbed his thumb over the blade. "This thing wouldn't cut hot butter," he said, and handed the knife, handle first, to Merryweather Handal. The general released Pete from his grip and examined the weapon.

"I suppose I will be forced to relinquish Mr. Turk of his duties," Handal said. "It's a pity that I have to fire men, but I abhor violence, except when performed in the name of righteousness or in my wonderful fiction. Pete, I trust I did not hurt you with my ironlike grip."

"I'll live, Colonel."

"General."

Goldman cleared his throat. "Well, if everyone's on a friendly basis now, I think I'll try to scrounge up some more firewood. Be seeing y'all."

As soon as the Missourian had disappeared, L. Merryweather Handal wagged a meaty finger in Belissari's face. "That," he said, "that is the kind of man I'm looking for, Pete, the kind of behavior I expected from a gentleman such as yourself. Instead of trying to kill a good man like Baron Van Hallstedt, a hero of the Franco-Prussian War, a man who is paying me good money to show him the West, you should act with honor like your friend Mr. Goldstein."

"Goldman."

"He's constantly gathering firewood. He's even escorting Bonaventura when she washes the dishes or laundry. He is a man of honor. You, Peter, should be ashamed of yourself."

"Yes sir," Pete said, and went to find Hannah.

The Turk disappeared.

When they woke up the next morning, they found him, a saddle, bridle, canteen, and one of the horses missing. Mr. Butterworth volunteered to go look for the wagon driver only to return a few hours later to say he lost the trail.

"Do you not hang horse thieves in this country?" Van Hallstedt asked.

"Sometimes," Pecos answered.

Pete muttered, "And we should hang horse killers." But no one heard him.

The broke camp after a noon meal and headed down the mountains toward the San Antonio–El Paso Road. Pete half-expected L. Merryweather Handal to blame Turk's desertion on him, saying if he hadn't fought with the wagon driver so much maybe they wouldn't be short-handed. And maybe, in his own way, Handal did by ordering Pete to drive Turk's wagon.

Pulling his hat low over his eyes, Belissari climbed

into the wagon, released the brake, and joined the train.

"Just two–three more days," he told himself. "Just two–three more days." After that, Baron Van Hallstedt and L. Merryweather would be Buddy Pecos's problem. And Hannah's.

Chapter Twelve

"If it makes you feel any better," Tom Rockwall told Pete, "I would have clubbed that uppity baron just like you did." Rockwall tapped the his pipe against a rock and stuck the stem in his mouth. He sat by the fire, long legs stretched out, and a leather-bound book in his lap. As Pete poured himself a cup of coffee, the driver closed the book and slid it into a canvas sack.

Waiting for the coffee to cool, Belissari squatted beside the black man. "Thanks," he said and, nodding at the sack, asked, "Good book?"

Rockwall shrugged. "Fair, I guess," he said after removing the pipe. "It's a history of the Franco-Prussian War. I'm what you might call an appreciator of military history, world history, from Hastings to the Little Bighorn."

"Franco-Prussia," Pete said, shaking his head. "I can't seem to escape it."

Tom Rockwall's spade beard parted, revealing the wagon driver's tobacco-stained teeth. He looked like a grinning porcupine. "Funny thing," he said, "this is about as thorough a book as you'll find on the war, and yet I find no mention of one Baron Van Hallstedt. You would think a self-styled hero would warrant at least a sentence or two. I mean, this book is six hundred and eighty-seven pages long."

Pete tested the coffee. Still a tad too hot. He shrugged. "Maybe the baron sees himself a hero, but historians don't."

"Or maybe . . ." Rockwall paused long enough to suck hard on the pipe, savor the taste for a few moments, send a blue cloud to mingle with the smoke from the fire, ". . . the good baron never served in the late war."

Belissari cocked his head, considering Rockwall's comment. "Maybe," was all he said. What did it matter? So Baron Van Hallstedt served as a foot soldier in the war. Or perhaps he didn't fight at all. Many men exaggerated their accomplishments on horses, hunting, fishing, fighting. If the baron stretched the truth a little, or even a lot, he would find plenty of company out here in Texas.

They chatted some more, enjoying tobacco and coffee, about a wide range of subjects including baseball, the battle of Troy, fishing in the Corpus Christi Bay, and their various professors in Louisville and Atlanta.

Hannah ended the conversation by ringing the iron tri-angle and declaring that supper was served.

Pete picked at the beans, biscuits, and salt pork. He didn't feel that hungry, and despite himself he couldn't get Rockwall's comment out of his mind. It festered like a dirty wound. It blossomed like a cactus after a desert rain. It grew like young Christopher. He forced himself to think of something else, but it came back like a hungry rat.

After supper, he dumped his dishes in the wreck pan and checked on the stock. Either Baron Van Hal-lstedt served in the Franco-Prussian War or he didn't. He was a hero, or he wasn't. Out here, it didn't matter one way or the other. You judged a man on how he acted, not on what he said he had done in the past, or even what you knew he had done.

Enough, he told himself.

Yet four minutes later, he stood beside Hannah as she washed the dishes and he dried them. "Tom Rock-wall told me something that got me thinking," he said.

"Oh."

"He's reading a history of the Franco-Prussian War, and there's no mention of a Baron Van Hallstedt in it."

He thought he caught Hannah rolling her eyes, but couldn't be certain. She handed him a tin cup. "I doubt if you'd find any history of the War Between the States that mentions Buddy Pecos. It doesn't mean he didn't fight."

"True." He put the cup on the tailgate of the wagon and accepted a plate from Hannah. "But it makes me wonder if the baron is who he says he is."

Hannah shook her head. "Petros, you're acting silly.

All right, let's say you're right, that the baron ran away from Prussia because he was a coward. He stowed away on a ship and landed in New York. He told everyone he had served in the war. It helped him get a job. He became rich. And no one knows the truth about his past except you and the good baron. Or make up some other tale. Who cares?"

Without commenting, he dried the plate furiously.

Hannah gave him another plate. "But . . . Lady Guinevere is no lady. I learned that while you were gone."

Now, Belissari rolled his eyes. "And what exactly did you learn?"

"She said her husband was killed in a certain battle, but Tom Rockwall told me that battle was fought in 1879. Her son is six years old. It doesn't add up."

Shaking his head, Pete stacked the dry plate on top of another. "Hannah," he said, "now you're talking like those white-haired ladies after Sunday worship." He paused. "Tom Rockwall told you this?"

"Yes, he was reading a history of the Zulu affair."

Belissari pursed his lips. "Mr. Rockwall reads a lot, doesn't he?"

Hannah shrugged. She gave him the coffee pot.

"You're washing a coffee pot?"

"The Klinks insist on it."

"Spoils the taste. Since when did you wash coffee pots?"

"Since Jones Handal told me that the Klinks insist I wash the pot and informed me that the Klinks are paying a great sum of money and if they want their coffee to taste like soap, so be it. Are you going to dry that pot or stand there like a stump?"

Belissari shook his head. "Buddy once shot a man for washing a coffee pot."

The July sun baked the San Antonio–El Paso Road as the wagon train meandered about the dusty trail toward Wild Rose Pass. Cheap grass swayed in the dips between juniper- and cactus-dotted hills beneath a cloudless blue sky. Except for the flowing creeks, you couldn't tell it had rained recently. Dust hung thick, silencing even the honorable Brig. Gen. L. Merryweather Handal, Esq.

Despite the heat, they made good time. Maybe the baron, Klints, and Lady Guinevere were making haste for a taste of civilization, if they would be so inclined to call dusty Fort Davis civilization. Well, the adobe town did serve as seat of the newly formed Jeff Davis County. Before that, it had been the Presidio County seat from 1875 until voters opted to move the government to Marfa in 1885. Travelers could find several hotels, more saloons, a bakery, even an ice house, tailor, and dairy. But no one would ever mistake Texas's "Mile High City" for Vienna or London.

Pete wondered if the Klints, Van Hallstedt, Schnitzler, Lady Guinevere, and Eugene would tell L. Merryweather Handal where he could take his troupe as soon as they reached Fort Davis. He couldn't blame them. Their hunting expedition had bagged one doe and one mustang stallion. And this was the country where, so the stories went, Bigfoot Wallace, while driving a stagecoach through Wild Rose Pass, shot a buck on top of a nearby mesa. The deer fell over the side and landed in front of the wagon, where Wallace blurted out, "These is the first mountains I seen where the game comes to heel after gettin' kilt."

They pulled off the road to make camp, stopping early to rest the animals, and the Klinks, because of the heat. Tomorrow afternoon, the train would pull into Hannah's ranch, and Belissari would wash his hands of Baron Van Horse-killer. Hannah could stay with them if she wanted the money that much. Anyway, she would probably rest easier knowing Pete was close by in case the orphans needed something.

"Are them ducks?"

Pete dumped a handful of grain on the ground in front of Buddy's horse. He glanced at Eugene, licking a peppermint stick, and turned to look in the direction the boy faced. Turkey vultures circled a cliff west of the road, far from the campsite. Probably over a dead or dying coyote or antelope. Maybe a calf, but he hoped that wasn't the case.

"No sir," he told the boy. "Those aren't ducks. Turkey vultures."

"Turkeys?"

Pete smiled. "Vultures. Nasty birds. You know what a buzzard is?"

"Nope."

"Well, they feed on dead flesh."

"You mean them birds eat dead things?"

"That's right."

Eugene's teeth broke the candy stick. He swallowed, still staring at the circling vultures. "Ain't that something? Can we go see what they're eating?"

Pete shook his head. "Too far."

"Don't look that far."

"Distances can fool you out here," he said. "Besides, you wouldn't want to miss supper, would you?" When the boy shook his head, Belissari smiled. "Good, you want to help me feed these horses?"

"No," he answered. "I detest manual labor."

And with that, he was gone, polishing off his peppermint candy as he ducked underneath the reata that served as a corral. Belissari scratched his head. He never considered himself erudite regarding the mind of a child, even though he lived around seven orphans, but Eugene left him more than a little perplexed. The kid didn't act like an only son in a British upper class family. He lacked his mother's accent. Most of the time, he was just like Desmond or Paco, a boy full of energy with too much time on his hands. But sometimes the kid acted just as snobbish as Baron Van Hallstedt or Doctor Ludwig Schnitzler.

"Where's Pete?" Hannah asked.

She had grown accustomed to Pete helping her dry dishes, but now Buddy Pecos stood in his place. After supper, she and Bonaventura had gone to the nearby creek to fill their canteens and wash the clothes of those paying guests. She felt like some old laundress at Fort Davis.

Buddy grunted something, turned his head to spit, and wiped his mouth with the back of his hand before answering. "Little Eugene run off. His mama was all worked up, but Pete said he taken a notion to where

the kid run off to, so they went after him. Ain't nothin'
to worry 'bout. Kid couldn't have gotten too far."

"Pete?" Hannah said. "And Lady Guinevere?"

"Yup."

She bit her tongue. "How nice." The sarcasm tasted
like brine in her mouth.

"Drink this," Pete said, handing the canteen to the
Englishwoman.

She drank greedily, and Pete pulled the canteen
away. "Not too much. Not too fast."

Guinevere wiped her mouth. "I'm sorry," she said
softly. "I was just so thirsty."

Belissari slammed the stopper into the canteen with
the palm of his hand, then wrapped the canvas strap
over his saddle horn. "This country will fool you," he
said. "You think you're doing fine, and then all of a
sudden you're dying of thirst."

"Eugene?" Her voice was a gasp, and Pete regretted
his statement.

"He'll be fine," he said. "Don't worry yourself over
nothing." He nodded toward the circling birds. "My
guess is he's underneath those turkey vultures." Guinevere's eyes widened. That didn't come out the way
he wanted it to, so he quickly explained, "Eugene
wanted to see what had those vultures' interest. I'll
say one thing for your son. He can certainly get
around."

She smiled, looking radiant, the color returning to
her face. "He takes after his late father," she said, "a
gallant, gallant man."

Belissari tried not to think about what Hannah had

told him. He grunted something, sounding more like Buddy Pecos than a college graduate, and helped the beautiful woman into her saddle. Then he swung aboard Jason and kicked him into a walk. They weaved around cholla, yucca, and basalt boulders, then leaned forward in the saddles as the horses lunged up a hillside covered with loose rock and dead cactus. As soon as they reached the top, Pete reined up and looked ahead. He saw Eugene, sitting on a boulder about a quarter of a mile below, so preoccupied with the swarm of turkey vultures, he didn't hear the two riders.

Lady Guinevere stopped her horse beside Pete's. He let her catch her breath and pointed at her son.

"He's a trooper," he said.

The redhead's lovely face turned into a horrible mask. She coughed out the words: "That . . . stench . . . is that . . . a javelina . . . or a skunk?"

For the first time, Pete's nostrils caught the reeking odor of rot and decay. He frowned suddenly, knowing.

"Neither," he said.

Chapter Thirteen

"**S**omething stinks, don't it?" Eugene, nostrils pinched with forefinger and thumb, told Pete as he dismounted a skittish Jason.

His mother, following the mustanger, scolded her son, and Belissari told both to wait, handing the reins to the six-year-old. After pulling his bandana over his nose and mouth, Pete wedged himself between a couple of boulders, watching all the while for snakes and scorpions, and pulled himself into a rugged clearing of loose lava rock and dead juniper branches. Moving over the basalt proved difficult in his moccasins. He didn't want to twist an ankle here, so he took his time, aware of the sweat dampening his brow and back of his shirt.

The turkey vultures camped at the base of a corduroy cliff dotted by the occasional yucca and century plant. He pulled the revolver from his holster and fired twice into the air, the echo deafening in the close confines. The carrion-eating birds took flight, their wings beating the hot air violently, and Pete moved closer to the face-down body at the base of the cliff. He returned the revolver to the holster and let out a heavy sigh.

He had hoped to find a cow, but knew it would be human. As Belissari neared the dead man, he felt the bile rising in his throat. He recognized the man's clothes first and the back of the man's head, undisturbed by the vultures.

Turk.

As much as Pete disliked the man, he didn't want to see him dead. And no one deserved the fate, left unburied in the rough country to feed vultures, ravens and wolves. Belissari leaned against the side of the cliff to catch his breath before examining the corpse. He noticed two bloody holes in Turk's back and knew instantly neither was the work of a vulture. The man had been shot in the back twice. Murdered. Pete backed away from the cliff and looked up, trying to piece together what had happened. Turk hadn't been killed here, not on horseback at least, and he had stolen one of Handal's mounts. The terrain here was too rough for a horse. More than likely he had been killed at the top of the cliff, or somewhere else, then tossed over the side to hide the body.

Not the best place to dispose of a murder victim, though. Too close to the main road. That meant the killer didn't know this country, didn't care, or was in too big a hurry. Pete thought about his options. He didn't dare haul Turk's body out now, not past Lady Guinevere and little Eugene. He couldn't put them through that shock. No, his best bet was to leave, head back to Fort Davis and return with the Jeff Davis County sheriff. But he couldn't leave the body like this. Animals would destroy any evidence the law might find, not to mention scatter Turk's bones by the time Pete could return. He studied the eroded base of the cliff. It angled in, like an amphitheater, and the dirt was loose.

He would cave it in, burying Turk's body, then cover it with basalt rocks he could carry. That would probably do the job, at least keep the wolves and vultures at bay long enough for him to return with the sheriff. Pete found a dead juniper branch and began digging at the cliff above Turk's body. The soil began to sprinkle down, then an avalanche covered the corpse's legs. Belissari lifted his bandanna enough to spit. Next, he moved gingerly around Turk and began prying the earth above the man's head.

"Hold it right there!"

The black hat cast a shadow over Mr. Butterworth's hard eyes. He stood about ten yards from Pete, the Colt steady in his right hand. *How could he manage to sneak up on me like that?* Pete thought. Butterworth waved the revolver's barrel.

"Toss that makeshift shovel away," he ordered, and Pete obeyed.

Butterworth moved easily across the rocks, motioning Belissari to raise his hands over his heads and back away from the body. His eyes left Pete just for an

instant to glimpse Turk's body, to recognize the corpse
and the cause of death.

"Looks like I caught you in the act," Butterworth
said at last.

"It's not how it looks," Pete said.

"Yeah. Right. Unbuckle that gunbelt with your left
hand, then back up."

Knowing better than to argue with a man with a
Colt aimed at his belly, Belissari followed the instruc-
tions. As Butterworth knelt to pick up the gunbelt,
Pete offered the truth. Butterworth didn't believe him.

"Let's go," he said. "You try to run, and I'll give
you what you gave Turk. Two bullets in the back. It's
more than you deserve."

Belissari gestured toward the corpse. "We should
finish burying the body. If we don't, wolves or vultures might destroy any evidence."

"I seen all the evidence I need to see. Move."

"Wow," Eugene exclaimed. "You mean he up and
murdered that fellow who run off on us."

"Yep," Mr. Butterworth said. "I caught him in the
act of burying the body. Lucky for you folks that I
come along. He might have killed the both of you,
too."

"Oh, my," Lady Guinevere said, covering her rosy
lips with her soft hands.

Butterworth swung into his horse and took the reins
to Jason. "You walk," he told Pete. Then to Eugene:
"Son, can you climb aboard the horse I'm leading?"

"Golly, you mean I get to ride him?"

His mother helped the boy into the saddle before

mounting her own horse. Butterworth told the Englishwoman: "I just came out here to help y'all find the
boy. I sure am glad I did."

"I didn't kill him," Pete said at last.

"Sure looks like you did," Butterworth said. "You
were fighting him all the time. You were trying to hide
the body when I caught you."

Pete cleared his throat. "You were the one who went
after him." He didn't hide the accusation in his voice.

"That's right," the gunman said. "But I lost his trail.
Reckon you didn't. You know this country better than
me."

"Just when did I have time to track him down, kill
him, and get back to camp? Remember, I was driving
Turk's wagon."

Butterworth smiled. "A man who wears Apache
moccasins is apt to be sneaky, quiet. But I'll leave that
to a judge and jury. Unless you try anything, mister.
Now start walking."

Nothing irritated a horseman more than to be afoot,
especially in this country. Especially when there was
a horse he could be riding. He slipped three times on
the loose rock as he headed uphill. No one said anything. Belissari longed for water but was too proud to
ask for any. He walked, the rocks cutting through the
thin soles of his moccasins, aware of the Colt Mr.
Butterworth kept trained on the small of Pete's back.
The sun had just begun to dip beneath the mountains
when they reached camp.

Hannah, setting the batter for tomorrow's breakfast,
looked up and wiped her hands on her apron. "Oh,
my," she said.

*   *   *

The honorable Brig. Gen. L. Merryweather Handal, noted scribe of the plains, friend to the noble red man, recorder of truth and real-life adventures, and Wild West escort, agreed that the evidence pointed directly at Pete Belissari, mustanger, murderer, but instead of hanging him here without the benefit of a trial he would insist on seeing justice played out through the Texas legal system. Sure, it would have taken some doing for Pete to sneak out of camp, track down Turk, kill him, dispose of the body, and make it back before anyone realized he was missing. But stranger things have happened, as anyone who ever read one of Handal's Five Cent Wide Awake Library classics knew.

No, Handal said, the right thing to do here, the only thing, really, was to take Pete to the sheriff and have him jailed for a murder most foul. Now perhaps Turk did deserve to be killed—after all, many Texans hanged horse thieves—but the code of the West, at least in Handal's literature, decried the shooting of anyone in the back, even Indians. So Pete must stand trial. Tom Rockwall bound Belissari's hands and feet and secured him to a wagon wheel. They would take turns guarding him.

Pete suggested they leave someone at Turk's body, to keep off the wolves. He nodded his head at Buddy Pecos, but Mr. Butterworth argued that Pecos was a friend of Pete's and might dispose of the evidence. He also ruled out Dave Goldman and Hannah, even L. Merryweather Handal. In turn, L. Merryweather Handal ruled out all of his paying customers as well as his wife. After all, no decent man would let his wife

look upon such a horrid scene, even though Jones
Handal informed him that she had seen worse, smelled
worse, and done worse. Baron Van Hallstedt said his
servant, Bonaventura, must not go because she was
needed here. So they asked for volunteers among Mr.
Butterworth, Tom Rockwall, Nehemiah, and Ramón,
all of whom politely but emphatically declined.

"So be it," Handal said, wiping his hands. "The
body of the late Mr. Turk stays as the murderer—"
his eyes shot in Pete's direction—"left him. We'll be
in Fort Davis tomorrow and turn this matter over the
the law. Mr. Butterworth, you have first watch."

Cup in both hands, Hannah knelt beside Pete and
offered him the coffee. She wondered if he would be
able to sleep like this, trussed up in a seated position
with a hemp rope around his chest securing him to the
left front wheel of what had been Turk's wagon. His
wrists and ankles were also bound tightly, but he could
grip the tin cup and bring it to his lips.

"Thanks," he said.

Hannah tried to think of something but came up
blank. Pete lowered the cup.

"You're looking at me as if you think I did it," he
said dryly.

She blushed and pushed the bangs from her eyes.
"Oh, Pete, you know me better than that. I know you
didn't do it." She tried not to smile. "Did you?"

He didn't think she was so funny.

"Petros, my love," she said, "this will work out.
You know it. You know there isn't a person in West
Texas who would believe you'd shoot anyone in the

back. No jury out here will convict you. We'll clear this up in no time. Besides, you wanted to shuck yourself of our merry troupe."

Pete tasted the coffee again.

Hannah glanced over her shoulder. Mr. Butterworth was the only one still awake, squatting by the fire and oiling a Winchester. She lowered her voice. "But who do you think did it?"

"Him." Pete nodded in Butterworth's direction.

"Really?"

"Who else could have done it? He went after Turk, said he lost the trail. My guess is he didn't. He murdered the arrogant little runt, then followed me when he saw the vultures, knew I'd most likely find the body. Pretty good plan, too. He frames me for the crime."

She thought about this for a few minutes. Pete drank some more coffee.

"But why?"

Belissari shrugged. "That I don't know."

Hannah wanted to look over at Butterworth but forced herself not to. She didn't want to arouse any suspicion. "It could have been anyone," she said. "Horse thieves. Bandits. We're not too far from Maggot's old headquarters in Horse Thief Canyon."

Pete shook his head. "We ran off old Maggot. Tore down his place. And he never was a murderer."

"No, but some of his customers were."

"But we haven't had any trouble with horse thieves, or rustlers for that matter, in a while. No, I'm certain that Butterworth did it. He's a gunman. What else do we know about him? Nothing. He did it."

"But how do we prove it?"

That stumped him.

"We need a motive."

He finished his coffee.

"You two lovebirds cut the gab," Butterworth said.

Hannah took the empty cup, kissed Pete on the forehead, and headed for the chuckwagon. Nothing would happen for a while. Butterworth, if he had killed Turk and framed Pete, wouldn't do anything else. She'd have to catch him, set up some sort of trap. But how?

Chapter Fourteen

Amos Ammons, duly elected as sheriff of Jeff Davis County back in March, took statements from everyone in Handal's group, then tossed Pete into the one jail cell that didn't have a broken lock. That meant dragging Curly Pedro Atacosa, sleeping off a drunk, into the neighboring cell.

A Tennessean by birth, Amos Ammons was fifty years old, looked forty, and acted fourteen. He had ridden with Bedford Forrest during the War Between the States until a cannonball demolished an oak tree and sent a heavy limb crashing against Sgt. Ammons' head. Folks said he was never quite right after that. But he was honest, and had been in Texas since drifting down from Kansas in the 1870s as a buffalo runner. He had even served as a Texas Ranger in the Hill

120

Country. One thing was certain. He'd make sure Pete got a fair trial.

"Circuit judge won't be here till next month," he told Hannah in a deep Nashville drawl, leaning back in his chair and resting his John Cubine boots, black with red kid leather tops, on the desktop. "Give y'all plenty of time to hire Pete a lawyer."

"Or," Hannah suggested, "find the real murderer."

"Yes'm. I'll send some of the boys out to bring in that dead dude's body. As soon as Harry's done a-cuttin' hair, I'll have him look over the body before we bury him at the county's expense. Let you know if we find somethin', Miss Hannah."

"Thanks, Sheriff."

"I warrant you'll be a-stayin' close till the trial."

Hannah shook her head. "No, I'll be riding out in the morning with General Handal."

"*What?*" This came from Pete's cell.

Hannah continued addressing Amos. "But we'll be back before the trial. With luck, you'll be able to turn Pete loose and arrest the real killer."

"Hannah!"

With a Davy Crockett grin, Sheriff Ammons placed his feet on the floor. His leather chair squeaked as he rose and picked up his wide-brim gray hat. "Reckon y'all got some talkin' to sort out. I'll run fetch Pete some supper. Now, don't take advantage of my friendliness. Iffen you let Pete out, I'll have to shoot him down like a mangy dog. And if Curly Pedro wakes up, tell him he can go on home. I'll collect the fine later."

He took the keys to the jail cell with him, opened the door and headed across the street. Hannah looked across the room. The only sound came from Curly Pedro, whose snores rattled the log building's windows. Pete, hands clenching the iron bars, glared at her. She walked toward him but decided to stay out of his reach.

"What do you mean you're going with Handal?"

"Hush," she told him. "You'll wake Curly Pedro."

He responded with a series of Greek words and phrases she was certain he wouldn't use in front of his mother. Hannah let him vent, then smiled. Sometimes, her smile had a calming effect on Pete, but not now. He barked some more. Curly Pedro mumbled something in Spanish and rolled over, covering his head with his dirty sombrero. His snores stopped briefly, quickly resumed. By then, Pete had fallen quiet.

"Petros, dear," she said, "listen to me. If this case goes to trial, we will need money for a lawyer, and Merryweather Handal is paying me seventy-five a month. Plus, this way I get to stay close to Mr. Butterworth. I'll find out how and why he killed Turk."

"We know how," Pete said. "He put two bullets in the man's back. And that means he probably will do the same to you."

"Pete, don't worry. Buddy and Dave will be with me."

"No. I forbid it."

Forbid? Hannah felt her own temper rising. She started to blurt out some of her own choice words and phrases, but just as suddenly she smiled. "How do you plan on stopping me, Petros?" she asked, and kicked a small pebble on the dusty floor through the iron bars. With that, she turned away as Pete yelled and yelled. Hannah didn't stop, didn't turn back. She opened the door just as Curly Pedro Atacosa sat up in his bunk and said, *"Señor, por favor.* I am trying to sleep."

Hannah closed the door behind her.

The honorable Brig. Gen. L. Merryweather Handal dropped by later that night bringing assurances to Pete that he, Handal, being an astute observer of Western men, knew for a fact that Belissari was innocent of Turk's murder, and that he, Handal, would indeed find the real culprit and bring him to justice, alive or, if need be, strapped over the back of a fine, high-stepping mustang stallion.

"Would you like to know who did the dirty deed?" Handal asked softly, apparently not wanting Sheriff Amos Ammons, intently focused on a game of solitaire chess but playing the game as if it were checkers, to hear.

"Sure," Pete said.

"Nehemiah."

Belissari blinked. Nehemiah. The little, bespectacled man who drove Lady Guinevere's wagon. The fellow you would never notice unless you tripped over him while he cleaned his lenses with a dirty bandana. Belissari waited for an explanation, but when it never came, he asked: "What makes you think he did it?"

"I'm glad you asked, Peter, my boy," Handal said in a hoarse whisper.

Ammons performed a double jump, black pawn over white pawn and knight, and told himself: "Crown me." Handal waited until the sheriff cleared his throat and concentrated on his next move.

"Are you sure you're safe with this lawman?" Handal asked.

Safer than Turk was with your crew, Pete thought, but said, "Amos is all right."

"Well, if you insist. Because, Pete, if it comes down to a hanging, I will not let you die like that. Dynamite is the key. If you are convicted, I will blast you out of this infernal hole." He clapped his hands loudly. "Boom! *Ka-boom!* The wooden shell of this building disintegrating into mere kindling as my friends and I ride by on trusty black steeds, firing wildly into the night, women and children screaming in terror of these demons in the dark. Boom! Ka-boom!"

"*Señors!*" Curly Pedro exclaimed.

"Shut up!" Sheriff Ammons shouted. "I can't concentrate on my game here with all that racket!"

Handal raised a finger to his lips and told Pete to be quiet.

"Anyway, Peter, it is Nehemiah. I've noticed he carries something in his trouser pocket."

"A case for his glasses," Pete said.

But Handal didn't seem to hear. "And I suspect it is a double-barreled Remington derringer. Two shots, I remind you, and two shots did in the poor Turk. Plus, I've noticed him following Lady Guinevere. And twice I've caught him in the wagon near her trunks, as if he were about to break in and rummage through her dashing wardrobe. What does that tell you?"

"Nothing," Pete said.

Handal nodded excitedly. "Exactly. It tells you that

Nehemiah is no wagon driver but a foul fiend prone to waylay helpless damsels and backshoot those who catch on to his evil ways." The writer's eyes widened. "This means that I, too, may meet the same fate as your dear old friend, Turk. But it's a chance I must take. Don't worry, Peter. Your day shall come and right will prevail. Good evening. Don't worry about me. And I shall protect your beautiful Hannah even if it means my death."

He spun around, tipped his hat at Sheriff Ammons, and left.

"You got friends, Pete," the Tennessean drawled. "You surely got a bushel of friends."

"Yeah," Pete said, adding quietly, "and with a friend like Handal, I just might hang."

After breakfast, Pete stood on his cot and peered through the small barred window. Handal's wagons stood in line down the dusty street, pointed southeast toward Mitre Peak. Ramón Armando drove the remuda down the quiet road, and Pete tried to follow the *vaquero* but lost sight of the Mexican and the horses soon. Still, he could see the rising dust and knew Ramón was driving the horses toward Alpine, not Marfa. That meant they would be heading toward the brutal country of the Big Bend, the Chisos perhaps, or maybe around Marathon, not the Chinatis, Shafter, or Presidio. The desert sun would be brutal, water scarce. It wasn't the place he wanted Hannah to be with a killer like Mr. Butterworth.

The bell above the telegraph office door rang, and a black man stepped outside and headed toward one of the wagons. Tom Rockwall. Pete scratched his head. What would Rockwall be doing in a telegraph office? Suspicion clouded his face. What did he know about this Rockwall, other than he said he had been a professor in Atlanta? And what was it Rockwall told Hannah he had been reading? A history of the Zulu wars—which had turned Hannah against Lady Guinevere. Well, she had been against the Englishwoman for a good while before that, but still . . .

And yet Rockwall told Pete he was reading a history of the Franco-Prussian War, and went on to cast some question on the veracity of Baron Van Hallstedt's war record. Just how many books did Tom Rockwall have with him? Come to think of it, Pete never actually saw the book. Had Hannah? He dropped onto the bunk and tugged on his mustache.

Tom Rockwall? Could he have killed Turk? Belissari shook his head. No, it had to be Butterworth. But . . .

And what about Nehemiah? What was he doing in the wagon near Lady Guinevere's trunks? A petty thief? A killer? Maybe Handal was right. Yet it didn't seem likely. The Englishwoman had probably asked Nehemiah to fetch something. He thought again of Baron Van Hallstedt, theorized how Turk, somehow, had discovered the good baron was a fraud, and Van Hallstedt murdered him. It could have happened. Or maybe Bonaventura? Perhaps Turk had spied on her, maybe had attacked her—that would be just like an Ottoman devil—and she killed him, shot him trying to defend herself, then panicked.

Pete swung his long legs onto the bunk and lay

down. What a stupid idea. Bonaventura. She didn't seem capable of hurting a spider. But maybe . . . Dave Goldman. Turk had attacked Bonaventura, and Goldman had killed him. No, Goldy would have owned up to it—unless he was protecting Bonaventura's honor. Sure.

Or Lady Guinevere. Turk had spied on her before. This time . . . no, he couldn't see that nice English lady shooting a man in the back twice, then letting Pete rot in jail for the crime.

Dr. Ludwig Schnitzler! He could have done it. What did Pete really know about the good pill-roller from Vienna? Nothing. Turk found out that Schnitzler was no doctor at all, but some phony, and that led to murder. Or . . . Jones Handal. She was a crack shot. She could have put two bullets into the wagon driver's back easily. Who would have suspected her?

Then there were the Klints, Gustave, Carl, and . . . he tried to think of the woman's name . . . Dagmar. Carl, always target shooting, and not a good marksman. He fired a few shots at what he thought was an antelope or deer or something, looked into the brush and . . . my gosh, he had killed Turk. So he panicked, got rid of the body, kept quiet. Maybe Butterworth had helped him. That would be something a gunman like that would do. Hide the body. Frame someone else. Then blackmail the Klints for the rest of their lives.

Or Gustave? Maybe Turk was blackmailing him, and Klint tired of it, tired of Turk, and killed him. Or his wife. Never underestimate a woman. Dagmar looked and acted weak, tired from the sun and altitude. But why would the altitude of the Davis Mountains bother a woman from Vienna? Six-thousand-foot-high mountains? Those were mere foothills to Europeans.

Pete sat up, thinking of the horses. Ramón? Why not? He could just as easily be a killer, even though Hannah said he couldn't cut the wounded doe's throat. Perhaps that had been an act, to throw off suspicion.

It could be anyone of them. Pete paused, eliminating Hannah, Buddy Pecos, Eugene, and Merryweather Handal. Unless the general shot the Turk by accident while in his cups.

Sheriff Amos Ammons cleared his throat. "I'm a-takin' Curly Pedro home," he said. "You need somethin' while I'm gone? Be back in an hour or so."

"No."

Amos pushed back his Stetson. "You don't look so good, Pete. You off your feet or somethin'?"

"My head hurts," Belissari said.

And it did hurt. He rested his right arm over his eyes, and never heard the wagon train pull out of town.

Chapter Fifteen

Once they continued south past Alpine, at Mr. Butterworth's suggestion, Hannah knew Pete had been right, that Handal's partner murdered Turk. Now, he was taking the party south, toward the Mexican border, through some of the roughest country in Texas. They could have traveled east toward Marathon, the town Captain Albion E. Shepard had started at a railroad water stop. The country between Alpine and Marathon seemed scenic enough, with less chance of trouble. But Mr. Butterworth suggested heading for the Big Bend of the Rio Grande to show off the Santiago, Chalk, Christmas, and Chisos mountains, and maybe some of the abandoned baronial forts.

That was all it took for Hannah Scott. To her reasoning, Mr. Butterworth would lead this party to the middle of nowhere, rob them, either kill or abandon them, and flee across the border into Mexico. Now all she had to do was wait for him to make his move, and then spring a trap on the cool, calculated killer.

She had better make plans with Buddy and Goldman.

The heat prevented much conversation and slowed their progress. Hannah began to wonder if they would be back in time for Pete's trial. Maybe that was Butterworth's plan, to prevent them from testifying on Pete's behalf. The country turned reddish orange, towering mountains bare of vegetation, iron-hard ground and only a few lizards sunning themselves. She had been in this part of Hades before, kidnapped three years ago by a bandit named Solomon Wooten and his gang. They hid out in the ruins of an ancient Spanish fort before Pete, like The Greek Gun of Handal's penny dreadfuls, came charging to the rescue.

That brought about another theory. Butterworth was leading them to the fort where Hannah had been held hostage, meaning that Butterworth had ridden with Solomon Wooten. Not in July of '84, of course. Hannah would have recognized him. But sometime before that. How else would he know about the fort?

She could theorize all day. Pulling her hat low over her eyes, Hannah flicked the reins and tried to pick up the pace a little in the chuckwagon. The quicker she trapped Mr. Butterworth, the sooner she and the rest of the troupe would be back in safer, cooler Fort Davis and Petros would be out of jail.

Over the past few days, Pete Belissari had read every wanted poster tacked on a board near the front door of the sheriff's cabin and jail. He had even taught Amos Ammons that chess wasn't quite played the same as checkers, but the sheriff didn't care much for the rules of chess so they opted to play blackjack. The Tennessean dealt Pete a jack down and a six up, but he showed a seven so Belissari asked for a card. It was the nine of hearts.

"Bust," Pete said, and reached through the bars to toss the cards facedown on the oak keg they used for a card table.

"Good thing we ain't a-playin' for real," Amos said, revealing his hand that totaled eighteen. "You'd owe me a right smart of money." He dealt Pete a four and a five. Pete asked for a card and was given a queen. Amos had a king showing. He took a card, the seven of hearts, and frowned.

"That busts me. Looks like you finally won a hand, Pete. It's a-gettin' long about noon. You hungry?"

Belissari nodded, although the thought of more burned salt pork, beans, and chicory coffee didn't do much for his appetite. Ammons gathered the cards and tossed the deck on his desk. He picked up his gray Stetson and told Pete he would be back in thirty minutes or so.

"Don't you run off nowheres," he said with a smile.

Why would anyone wish to leave such glorious accommodations? Belissari said to himself as he looked over his surroundings one more time. When had Amos Ammons cleaned out his office, cleaned off his desk, or emptied the trash can in the corner of the building? The place was a regular tinderbox. And what about those old wanted posters?

"Sheriff," Pete called out. When Ammons turned around at the door, Belissari pointed to the reward poster.

"Plomo is dead," he said. "Don't you think you should take it down?"

Amos chuckled and stared at the yellowing poster. He jerked it off the board, folded it in half and tore it into strips which he dropped in the kindling bucket near the stove. "You know," he said, "I could bring you a Bible or something if you've got a hankerin' to do some readin'. Maybe one of those funny books you's always a-readin'. That sound good?"

"Yeah," Pete answered with enthusiasm. "There should be a book of Homer in my saddlebags."

"I'll see what I can do." He closed the door, and Pete listened to the jingling spurs as Ammons crossed the street and headed for Lempert's Addition for some grub.

Belissari went to his cot, pulled himself up to look through the barred window. Town was quiet on this day. He tried to remember what day it was. Sunday? Monday? He wasn't sure. Maybe Amos would bring him a newspaper. He dropped back down, sat on his bed, and ran fingers through his long hair. He could use a bath and a shave, not to mention some clean clothes. Bored. How bored could a man get? Now he had gotten to the point where he looked forward to playing blackjack twice a day and reading wanted posters he had memorized.

That reminded him of the poster Ammons had torn down. Pete crossed the small cell and leaned against the bars, straining his eyes in the dark building to read the poster the placard on Plomo had hidden.

ONE THOUSAND DOLLARS
REWARD
IN GOLD COIN!!!!!
Wells, Fargo & Co.
WILL PAY
ONE THOUSAND DOLLARS
for the apprehension
DEAD OR ALIVE
of Horace Wilbur Butterworth,
alias J. B. Butterfield, Killer Will, Will Worth
Wanted for Robbery and Murder.
On August 18, 1883, Butterworth stopped
the Danville stage and took the Treasury Box,
then killed the messenger and a passenger
in the state of Missouri.
Killer is also wanted for assault, horse theft,
rustling, fraud and stealing a sow.
J. J. Valentine, Gen'l Supt.
Rideout, Smith & Co., Agents

There was no mistaking the sketch of Mr. Butterworth. Pete's knuckles tightened against the iron bars until his arms shook.

"Ammons!" he shouted. "Sheriff Ammons! Somebody let me out of here!"

They pitched camp in a basin flowered with ocotillo and bordered by mountains that resembled something out of a Jules Verne novel. The locals called it Outlaw

Hole, but as far as Hannah knew, no outlaws had ever stayed there. It wouldn't be much of a hideout with a name like that. But it offered shade and, most importantly, a shallow pool of rainwater caught by an eroded bed of hard rock. Hannah's eyes followed Butterworth as he and Ramón walked to the horse herd. Only when she was certain he had traveled out of hearing distance—and noise carried far in this country—did she speak to Buddy and Goldman.

"You'll have to keep a close eye on him," she told Buddy. "This is his game now."

Pecos nodded. "You're for certain he's our man?"

"I'm certain."

The sharpshooter's one eye locked on Goldman. "I'll keep a lookout here anyway," Goldy said, "in case he's got a partner or he slips by you."

"He ain't slippin' by me," Pecos stated flatly.

At Butterworth's request, Pecos was to lead a hunting party at first light tomorrow in search of a mountain lion. Butterworth would go with him, and Jones Handal interjected that she had a hankering for some cougar meat and offered to join them. Nehemiah would drive a wagon and be the camp cook in case it took longer than a day. The customers on this jaunt would be Carl Klint, Dr. Schnitzler, and young Eugene. Not that the boy would be hunting. Against a mountain lion? Too dangerous. But his mother thought that going out alone with the menfolk (and she must have included Jones Handal with this lot) would be a fine adventure for him to tell his friends back in London.

Hannah filled their stomachs with sourdough biscuits and fried potatoes the next morning, and watched them disappear over the rise. Two hours later, Gen. L. Merryweather Handal shouted that the dirty fool Nehemiah had taken the wagon with all of their hunting arms and ammunition.

"By Jupiter!" he thundered, "we are left alone to fend for ourselves in this country most dangerous and deadly. Who has a weapon? My kingdom for a weapon!"

Dave Goldman carried a Smith and Wesson .44 Russian, and Handal had a .41 Remington derringer. "How about you, sir?" the novelist asked Tom Rockwall.

"No, sir," the wagon driver replied. "Sorry, but I do not own a firearm."

Slapping his dusty hat against his dusty thigh, Handal coughed at the powdery dust and shook his head. "Any rifles?"

No answer.

"Shotguns?"

"Everything is in the wagon," Gustave Klint said.

Handal scratched the cleft in his chin. "Nehemiah," he said dryly.

And Hannah began to wonder if maybe the honorable brigadier general, esquire, had been right. Nehemiah was their man, not Mr. Butterworth. Or perhaps he was working for the killer. In any case, they were, basically, left unarmed. One revolver and a two-shot derringer wouldn't offer much protection. Still, they had plenty of food and water. And horses.

The livestock, and Ramón Armando, disappeared that night.

* * *

"That's him," Pete argued, jabbing his finger at the sketch on the poster Sheriff Ammons held. "That's Butterworth, the man with General Handal." His elbow banged against the iron bars, and he jerked his arm through the door and stifled a curse, clutching the elbow, while the Tennessean shook his head and scratched behind his right ear.

Ammons had been joined by the mayor of Fort Davis, one grizzled *vaquero* and former Sgt. Major Cadwallader. All three men studied the placard for a minute while Belissari waited for the pain in his elbow to subside.

"Well," the sheriff drawled. "I don't know."

The mayor squinted through his bifocals and pushed up his bowler. "Just because he has the same name—"

Pete cut him off. "He has the same face."

Ammons scratched behind his other ear like some blue-tick hound. "Does bare a fair to middlin' resemblance to that gent."

This was getting nowhere. Cadwallader cleared his throat and suggested that perhaps the sheriff should form a posse, just to be safe.

"Posse costs the county money, and we've only been a county since March. I'd hate to spend recklessly."

"Maybe you should go," Cadwallader said. "Alone."

"Then who'd look after the prisoner?"

"Your deputy?" the old buffalo soldier suggested.

"I ain't hired one yet. New county and all."

The mayor's pale head bobbed beneath the oversize

bowler. "Perhaps we should wait until General Handal returns. Then we can have this whole matter straightened out."

Pete stood dumbfounded. Everyone, even the intelligent Cadwallader, nodded in agreement. They didn't realize that Butterworth had no intention of returning to Fort Davis. The sheriff escorted the mayor and old soldier outside, talking now about the weather and recent rains. The *vaquero* stopped to roll a cigarette.

The idea hit Belissari quickly. "*Hombre*," he said, nodding at the pack of Bull Durham. "*Por favor*."

With a bow, the Mexican finished the cigarette and handed it to Pete. "*Gracias*," Pete said, and waited as the old man struck a Lucifer against his chaps and held the match near the bars. Pete puffed until the cigarette caught and sat on the bunk. With a smile, the *vaquero* rolled another smoke for himself and walked outside to join the fools.

Belissari took another drag on the cigarette. He coughed. He waited about a half-minute, then hurried to the edge of his cell, reached through the iron bars and flicked the smoke across the room. He had only one chance, but that's all he needed. The cigarette landed against the mountain of papers and old coffee grounds bubbling out of the sheriff's trash can and rolled out of sight.

Chapter Sixteen

It didn't take long for the shrieking to get on Hannah's nerves. Dagmar Klint wailed and wailed, and her wails echoed off the hard-face mountains, so she walked over to the wagon where Gustave gently shook his wife's shoulders and pleaded with her to calm down. Hannah reared back and slapped the lady silly.

"Be quiet!" she snapped, and Mrs. Klint obeyed. Gustave stared blankly.

Aware of the attention on her, Hannah spun around: "We have to stay calm. You lose your head in this country and you're as good as dead. We have water, we have food and shelter and we have eight rounds of ammunition."

Dave Goldman frowned. "Well, Hannah, I only keep five loads in my Russian."

138

"But it's a six-shooter!" Gustave Klint wailed, doing a pretty good imitation of his high-strung wife.

"Safety," Goldy explained sheepishly. "You know. Hammer on an empty chamber."

"Seven rounds, then," Hannah said. "If we use them only when we . . ." Her voice trailed off as Merryweather Handal shifted his big feet.

"General?"

"Well, I have the derringer, but no bullets."

Hannah dug her fingernails into her palms to keep from cursing or charging the novelist and choking him to death. "Mr. Handal," she said, staring at the hack writer's feet, "when you were . . . why did you say you had a weapon when you didn't have any bullets?" She didn't wait for an answer. She wasn't sure Handal would have one, and she knew she didn't care to hear it. Lifting her head, meeting the eyes of everyone except the Klints, who stood behind her, Hannah said, "Five shots. That's enough."

She studied the faces. Lady Gluebait looked rather pale. Worried about her son, perhaps? No, she had never shown anything for the boy during the entire trip. Why would she start now? Bonaventura had moved closer to Dave Goldman, feeling safer next to him. Rockwall silently, solemnly smoked his pipe. He'd be solid throughout any ordeal. The baron held his mouth open, in disbelief, shock or fly-catching. Handal's face had turned ashen like a man suddenly aware of just how far he was from the nearest barrel of peach brandy.

"Who are you talking about?" Lady Good-for-nothing asked. "What about my son? And why have they done this?"

"I think they want to leave us stranded so they can make a run for the border," Hannah answered. "I'm sure Eugene is all right." She didn't see any reason to bring up Turk's murder. "We know Ramón is one of them," she went on. "And I'm pretty sure he's working with Butterworth."

"Butterworth?" Handal looked perplexed. "What about Nehemiah?"

She wanted to pull out all of her hair. Maybe Nehemiah was in on the crime, maybe he wasn't. Right now, it didn't really matter. They way she figured it, Butterworth would either ditch the hunting party or try to leave them stranded the way Ramón had fixed them. Without horses, the party would have a long, hot walk back to civilization, and Butterworth and Ramón would have an easy ride to the border. She doubted if they would return here. So Hannah would make sure everyone filled canteens and anything else that could hold water. They'd move out. South, she figured, to the Rio Grande. Once there, they could follow the river west until they reached Presidio, inform the Rangers, and rent or buy horses and/or wagons to return home.

Then she heard the faraway report of a gunshot.

If he knew Amos Ammons, the sheriff would finish his discussion with the mayor at Lightner's Saloon. Pete only hoped Ammons would have more than one beer. He stared intently at the wooden trash can, waiting, praying, holding his breath. After a minute, he began to think, *a watched pot never boils*. Maybe the cigarette had gone out. After all, the can held coffee grounds, tobacco juice, and who knew what else. Yet a minute later, he caught the faint outline of rising smoke drifting toward the ceiling.

Pete let out his breath slowly, inhaled deeply. Waiting. Waiting. How much longer?

The fire erupted, almost exploded, and Belissari smiled as the orange flames danced, crackled. The white smoke turned black as the wood can caught fire, and soon the flames licked their way up the far wall. It spread like a grass fire, eating its way to the rafters and across the floor toward the sheriff's desk, devouring everything in its path.

Perfect.

Belissari suddenly frowned. *Perfect*? It quickly occurred to him that he hadn't thought this plan through very well. The idea was for Amos Ammons to return, see the fire, and realizing the danger, hopelessness, release Pete from the jail. Once outside, Belissari would overpower the sheriff and steal the closest, and best, horse on the street. It seemed brilliant, flawless, when Pete saw the *vaquero* rolling his smoke. But as the room filled with smoke, he began to understand the drawbacks. The idea seemed more like some far-fetched scheme straight out of the plot of one of L. Merryweather Handal's novels.

What if Amos never returned?

He spun around, jumped on his cot and pulled himself to the barred window. "Help!" he screamed at the deserted street. "Fire!" A Greek *táma* followed a

Texas curse. He raised his voice even louder. "Get me out of here. Fire! *Fire!* There's a fire in the jail!"

Smoke began to fill the cell, rushing through the window. Coughing, he dropped to the cot, underneath the smoke, tried to think of another plan. The keys! They rested on the peg near the board full of wanted posters, well out of his reach, where the keys always were. The fire began moving toward his cell, following the thickening smoke. Maybe once it burned through the floor, he could drop through the hole and scramble underneath the jail before the building collapsed on him. Maybe . . . but unlikely.

The door opened, and Amos Ammons raced inside, stopping suddenly at his burning desk.

"Sheriff!" Pete jumped up and gripped the warm iron bars. "Get me out of here!"

"Fire!" Ammons shouted.

"Fire!" Belissari confirmed. "Now get me out of here."

Shielding his face from the leaping flames, Ammons backed toward the peg that held the keys. He grabbed them, shrieked, and gripped his burned hand as the hot iron ring clattered on the floor. "Too hot!" Ammons yelled. The Tennessean looked up, eyes wide. "Every man for hisself! Abandon ship. Save what you can and get out!" He stuffed a package of chewing tobacco in his trouser pocket, lifted a brass spittoon and ran outside, the door slamming shut behind him.

Pete stared at the door with his mouth open . . . understanding just how bad his escape plan was and wondering which would kill him first, fire or smoke.

The heat seemed to suck what little oxygen the

cabin held, and he found himself on his knees, fighting for breath, smoke hanging over him like a shroud. This was it, he realized, and then he felt the flames shift direction, pulled by air. A draft of some sort.

"Mr. Belissari!"

Cadwallader! Pete rose slightly. "Over here," he said. "In the cell."

The wiry old trooper had come through the side door that led to the alley. Out front, a crowd had gathered to watch the fire, now hopelessly burning out of control. Only the old sergeant major had the courage to try to rescue Pete from a grisly death.

"Where are the keys?" he yelled, squatting next to Belissari.

Pete coughed, motioned carelessly toward the front door, now engulfed in an angry inferno. Cadwallader swore and stood, unbuttoning the flap on his military issue holster. "Stand back," he ordered, drawing the revolver even as he spoke, thumbing back the hammer, aiming and firing before Belissari barely moved.

Part of the roof collapsed over the sheriff's desk, muffling the shot. Cadwallader yanked on the iron door, cursed when it didn't budge, fired again. This time when he pulled, the heavy door swung open. Belissari tried to stand, realized he couldn't, and felt the soldier lift him, practically throw him down the short hallway. His eyes burned from the smoke, but he could make out the light from the alley. He burst through the thick black wall and wheezed, dropping to his knees in the dust, fighting for breath.

"No time for that, sir," ordered Cadwallader, right behind the horseman. He again helped Pete to his feet, pointed a long finger at Jason, saddled and waiting beside the soldier-turned-rancher's black Morgan.

Belissari's mind cleared. Cadwallader hadn't planned on rescuing Pete from a burning building. He had organized a jail break. Pete wiped his face with the back of his arm, saw his red shirt sleeve blackened by soot. He grabbed Jason's reins and pulled himself into the saddle.

"Thought you didn't believe me," he said, not sure if he made sense, uncertain even if his rescuer heard him.

"Sir, you must think I'm a fool," Cadwallader snapped, and slapped Jason's rump.

The two men galloped down the short alley, their horses sliding in the main street as the spurred past the saloons south of the town square. Behind them, Amos Ammons and a crowd of twenty or thirty people stood watching the jail collapse and send an Independence Day display of sparks flying skyward. No one paid any attention to the two riders heading out of town.

They slowed their horses only slightly on the road to Alpine, and didn't stop until they reached Mitre Peak. The ancient *vaquero* who had given Pete the cigarette sat on a zebra dun, puffing patiently on another smoke while about twenty head of stringy longhorns lazily searched for sparton grass along the rocky soil between the towering mountain shaped like a bishop's peaked hat and the winding road.

"Mr. Belissari," Cadwallader said, gesturing at the Mexican. "This is *Señor* Muñoz."

Belissari nodded slightly at the old-timer, who

flicked the remains of his cigarette into a pile of boulders. "We've met," Pete said.

"Yes. And I must remind myself to inform Mr. Muñoz never to roll you a smoke."

Pete couldn't disagree at the moment. The Mexican began speaking to Cadwallader in rapid Spanish, while Pete, every five or ten seconds, looked over his shoulder, certain to see Ammons leading a fast-shooting posse. He wished the two men would finish this conversation.

"All right," Cadwallader said. "Pete, we're going to drive these cattle toward Harris Owen's spread. After all, they're his beeves." The *vaquero* quickly began riding among the longhorns, twirling a lariat, forcing the cattle laying down, resting in the afternoon sun, to rise and start moving east.

"A cattle drive?" Pete snapped. "Pretty soon Amos is going to figure out I didn't burn to death in that jail, and there'll be a posse breathing down our necks."

"Exactly," Cadwallader said. "But Ammons likes to move slowly. He'll wire the marshal in Marfa and the Rangers down in Presidio. I'm betting he won't get started until tomorrow morning. So we'll lose our tracks with these mossy horns."

Belissari shook his head. "Waste of time."

"Pete, you got a lot to learn about being on the owlhoot." He raised his hand to stop any objection. "We drive these cattle, all three of us, for about a mile. Then *Señor* Muñoz and I leave you with the beeves and make a mad dash toward Alpine. Your Rebel sheriff isn't a complete fool. He'll realize our tracks disappear with the cattle, so he'll follow the trail. When he sees two horses leaving, he'll guess it's you and your savior."

Cadwallader's dark eyes gleamed. "*Savior*. I like the sound of that. You'd be well-done brisket if it weren't for me. Yes sir, I'm going to enjoy this." He began cutting his horse back and forth, pushing the longhorns into a tight bunch, explaining as he worked. Pete joined the work.

"Anyway," Cadwallader called out over his shoulder as the small herd crossed the road and dipped into an arroyo. "The posse will take after us. You keep the herd going about another mile or so, then light out."

Pete rounded some scrub brush and chased a brindle longhorn into the herd. He had to admit it. He liked Cadwallader's plan.

"Now," the former soldier continued, "after we're gone, you're on your own, mister. Muñoz and I will try to lose Ammons and his group between Marfa and Shafter, but we might have to make a run all the way to Mexico. You'll have to track down Butterworth alone. And remember this: Every lawman between Fort Stockton and El Paso will be looking for you. Steer clear of settlements. Don't forget you're charged with murder. The Rangers are likely to shoot you on sight. And considering that you burned down our new county sheriff's office and jail, so will the Fort Davis posse. Be careful, son." The last sentence came as a shock. Sgt. Major Cadwallader, showing concern for Pete?

"Thanks," Belissari called out. "Thanks to both of you. It's a good plan, Sergeant Major."

Cadwallader's cackle carried over the lowing of the

longhorns. "Well, it's better than burning down the jail with you locked inside a cell." The *vaquero*, who must have understood English, howled at this. "Pete Belissari, arsonist," Cadwallader said. "I like the sound of that, too."

Chapter Seventeen

A man alone. As a mustanger, Pete Belissari had spent months by himself, but that had been by choice. Now as he dodged the scattered settlements between Fort Davis and the Rio Grande, he felt like some starlight rider. He rode the zebra dun of the *vaquero*. They had swapped horses just before Muñoz and Cadwallader left the cattle and raised dust toward Mexico, the ex-buffalo soldier explaining that the sheriff might have a good tracker who would recognize Jason's prints. Once Pete loped away from the longhorns, he traveled at night, riding hard his first day on the run (after abandoning the beeves), now trying a steady, but less draining pace.

He carried Cadwallader's Spencer carbine in the saddle scabbard and, stuck in his waistband, an old .44 Remington cap-and-ball model that had been con-

verted to take modern cartridges. The Mexican's saddlebags held plenty of oats for the horse and one
half-eaten sandwich and several slices of beef jerky
for the rider. Belissari's stomach growled, but that
could be ignored. Pete would rather have oats for the
zebra dun than a thick steak for supper followed by a
shot or two of ouzo. Give a horse some oats, even if
just a handful to go with hay or whatever the animal
could forage, and it would last substantially longer
than one whose diet consisted only of grass.

Still, as he rode in the darkness south of Alpine, he
knew the dun was playing out. He rested most of the
afternoon in a cave, then mounted and picked his way
to a well-watered canyon that held plenty of Edward
L. Gage's Alpine Cattle Company horses. Already
charged with murder, and by now jail break and arson,
Pete saw no reason not to add horse theft to the list.
Besides, he'd be leaving Gage a pretty good horse in
exchange. A fair swap, he figured, and picked out a
buckskin mare.

The danger would be if one of Gage's waddies
checked on the horses and saw the zebra dun. Pete
didn't believe anyone would put the *vaquero*'s horse
with the jail break, unless Ammons sent a posse mem-
ber trailing the longhorns just to make sure. But Edward Gage might not think the swap was rightly fair,
and then Pete would have a Alpine Cattle Company
posse to dodge in addition to Amos Ammons . . . and
the Presidio County sheriff . . . and the Texas Rangers
. . . and maybe some bounty hunters. He had better
find Mr. Butterworth and Hannah soon, before the
whole country came down on him hard.

Twice, the buckskin tried to throw him before she finally settled down. Skittish after not being ridden for months, the mare bucked, startling the other horses in the canyon, but Belissari kept his seat. It reminded him of the Pecos rodeo just a few weeks earlier. Pete let the mare act up, getting the orneriness out of her system before kicking her into a canter. He headed south.

Belissari called the mare Penelope, after Odysseus's faithful wife. A handsome mare like this buckskin, feisty, short-coupled, fourteen hands high, and whose only problem seemed to be a wolf tooth in her upper jaw, was sure to have many stallion suitors. And, after the two short bucking spells, the mare proved faithful to Pete. He had picked the best horse in the canyon, but that didn't surprise him.

He guessed Butterworth's course, and guessed right. They had talked about showing the Europeans the ruins of old baronial forts and missions, and Belissari knew of a large one in the middle of the Big Bend. It had been outlaw Solomon Wooten's hideout in Texas before Pete helped end that reign of trouble, and it made sense—at least to Belissari—that Butterworth would want to go there. It was well-hidden, the only occupants tarantulas, coyotes, and rattlesnakes, and on the way to the Rio Grande, Mexico, and safety from Texas prosecution. They had a few days' head start, but they'd be lumbering along with wagons. Pete had a good horse, and when he found the trail, he knew it would be a matter of time before he caught up with the crew.

* * *

The black hat gave him away. Butterworth topped the rise on his horse and rode steadily toward Hannah and the others in Outlaw Hole. A couple of hours had passed since she heard the first gunshot, followed by a handful of others, and somehow Hannah realized the gunman would return here after all. He was alone. Good. Once he rode into the camp, Dave Goldman would shoot the scoundrel dead. Well, maybe not. Perhaps, he'd just get the drop on Butterworth. Or better yet, Handal could pull out his derringer. The killer would have no way of knowing the hideaway gun was empty. Merryweather Handal and Dave Goldman, their only hope.

"We're doomed," Hannah whispered.

She gasped, recognizing a bouncing figure in front of Butterworth. Eugene! The killer held the boy easily, smiling, using a six-year-old for a shield. He reined up easily and clutched the squirming boy.

"Eugene!" his mother shouted and ran toward the horse and riders, but Tom Rockwall reached out and stopped her as Butterworth drew his Colt and pressed the barrel against the boy's temple. Lady Guinevere screamed and fainted.

"Mama!" the boy shouted, struggling against the killer's ironlike grip.

"Anybody packing iron," Butterworth said, "had best toss it out in the open."

L. Merryweather Handal stepped forward, hands on his hips, and barked, "What is the meaning of this?"

The Colt shifted directions and boomed. Butterworth's horse sidestepped a little at the report but the killer regained control easily. Handal looked at the hole in the crown of his hat, still seated on his enormous head, and quickly found the empty Remington and pitched it. Hannah turned to Goldman, nodded, and the Missourian reluctantly unholstered the Smith and Wesson and threw it to the ground.

"Good," Butterworth said.

"Where's Buddy?" Hannah asked. "Where are the rest of them?"

Mr. Butterworth released Eugene, who dropped from the saddle and ran, not to his unconscious mother, but to pick up the derringer and revolver. Hannah started to call out, afraid the gunman would shoot the boy dead, but Butterworth merely smiled and holstered his Colt. Eugene checked the Remington, laughed and said, "It's empty, Horace."

"Don't call me that, boy," Mr. Butterworth said.

At that moment, Lady Going-Straight-To-Hades-As-Soon-As-Hannah-Could-Send-Her-There tore herself from Rockwall's grasp and walked easily to the gunman and boy. Eugene handed her the Russian revolver, and she cocked it deftly and turned to face the captives.

Hannah called the woman and her son a couple of dirty names.

"Ain't that the truth," Dave Goldman added.

Bonaventura said something in Italian and crossed herself. The baron demanded what was the meaning of all of this. Dagmar Klint fainted dead away, but, unlike Lady Graft, she didn't appear to be faking.

"Where is my son?" Gustave Klint yelled.

"Give up the act, Klint," the Englishwoman said. "We know who you are."

Hannah cleared her throat. "Do you mind telling us who all of *you* are?"

Two days into the desert, the mare went lame.

"This isn't faithful, Penelope," Belissari whispered to the mare.

Pete poured a little water from the canteen into his hat and let the buckskin drink. Afterward, he pulled the wet hat low, letting the dampness cool his head. He had water, a Remington and Spencer, plenty of oats and some jerky. But the Alpine Cattle Company mare wouldn't be chasing down anyone for quite a while. She had thrown a shoe on the rocks and now limped hopelessly.

Staring into the arid wasteland, Belissari considered his chances. He could turn back, head out, traveling at night and, with luck, reach Marathon or Alpine where he would be sure to be captured. Or he could head back toward the canyon where he had stolen the mare and grab another horse. Or luck upon some sheepherder who had a mule or maybe even a horse to trade.

Belissari gathered the reins and led the mare deeper into the desert, not out of it. He knew some of the water holes out here. As long as they hadn't dried up, hadn't become poison, he still had a chance to find Hannah and the others. If he went back, even if he wasn't caught, Butterworth would escape, and Pete didn't want to think about what he might do to Hannah and his friends. The man had killed before—at least twice during the stage holdup mentioned on the wanted poster, plus Turk—and he could only hang once.

Belissari was too far to make Outlaw Hole, but Novena Spring usually held water. Besides, he knew it better than Outlaw Hole. Back in '83, Pete had trapped mustangs at Novena Spring. It would be a long, hot walk, but once there, maybe he could snare a rabbit for supper, get a good rest, and head on toward the fort where he was certain Butterworth would hold up.

The sun dried out his hat quickly. His feet ached from the sharp rocks and prickly pear. He saw nothing, not even a vulture or a lizard, and heard only the wind, his footsteps, snorts from the horse, and the clopping of the mare's hooves on the hard ground. The smart move would be to find some shade and rest now, travel at night, but Pete didn't want to give Butterworth anymore of a head start. He could reach the spring before sundown, drink, rest, leave the buckskin at the water, and move on at night.

After traveling two miles, Pete rested again, pulled a piece of jerky from the saddle bags, and ate. He loosened the cinch, thought about leaving the saddle behind to ease the load on the mare but decided against it. He might need the saddle if somehow, some way, he came across another horse. He laughed at himself. Another horse? Out here? Glimpsing at the blinding sun, Pete wondered if sunstroke had begun to take hold. He uncorked the canteen and drank only a swallow. The mare snorted, but she'd have to wait. She had already had some water, and Pete knew it was best to conserve. Novena Spring might be dry.

Yet he wasn't scared. He knew this country, knew

its dangers. But he also could survive here, find water. In fact, he had everything figured out. By tomorrow morning, he would be shadowing Horace Wilbur Butterworth, waiting to spring a trap. His plan sounded logical.

But . . . so had setting the trash can on fire in the sheriff's office.

"Come on, Penelope." He tugged on the reins. The mare didn't resist and followed Pete down a steep, rocky incline dotted by waving ocotillo. Pulling the buckskin uphill proved a little harder, but they made it, the horseman slipping only twice, and man and rider causing a small avalanche that sent dust drifting with the wind. At the top of the hill, Pete caught his breath and patted the mare's neck.

"That's the worst of it," he told her. Penelope tried to bite his leg, but Belissari dodged away, smiling at the mare's friskiness.

Then he heard the faraway report of a gunshot.

Chapter Eighteen

Hannah's head hurt from trying to sort everything—
and everyone—out. Eugene wasn't Lady Gun-In-Her-
Hand's son. He was eight years old, not six, "young
and short for my age," he said, and hailed from Brook-
lyn. Guinevere, or whatever her name was, picked him
up off the streets, and the two had conned their way
to Chicago. There, the lady recognized Dagmar Klint.
It seems the two had worked together in a sordid little
house in Albany a few years back, so when she realized that Dagmar was posing as some woman of
means from Germany or Vienna or wherever she said
she was from, well, Guinevere resumed her English
accent and sought out Brig. Gen. L. Merryweather
Handal, Esq. Even the incident at the Pecos rodeo had
been planned, to make Handal and the others feel sorry
for the widow and her son.

"You see," explained Mr. Butterworth, gun in hand, "Gustave Klint's real name is Ranier Moritz. Pinkertons, U.S. marshals, half the law west of the Mississippi is looking for him. And for good reason. He was vice president of the Chicago National Bank, only a few months back he made off with, according to the papers, a tad short of four hundred thousand dollars."

Handal whistled.

"That's what I thought," Butterworth said. "Now, all I knew was that this Moritz gent had a partner, and both of them talked foreign. So when I seen Handal and his gang trotting south for Texas, I naturally joined up. Pretty good cover, I got to give you credit for that, Moritz."

Gustave Klint, or whoever he was, seethed.

"Traveling with a Buffalo Bill faker, going easy, taking your time, seeing the country. No one would ever suspect you to escape that way." Butterworth wet his thin lips, smiled, and continued. "My only problem was there was four foreigners here, and I wasn't sure who was the embezzlers, Gustave and Carl, or Doc Schnitzler and the baron."

Van Hallstedt cleared his throat. "I am no embezzler, sir," he said angrily.

"And you ain't no baron neither. Your doctor friend finally told me what I needed to know. Doc Ludwig is better known as Doctor Nepomuk Barthélemy who's been selling some snake oil to stupid sodbusters in Kansas and Nebraska. Only it seems that he put too much strychnine in one batch and left two folks deader than dirt. Baron, the way I see it, you just hooked up with Doc Bart at the wrong time. Baron Van Hallstedt is really Barry Deon, thespian. Pretty good, from what I hear, until he hit the scamper juice too much. According to the wanted posters, our baron had joined up with Doc Bart to help peddle that poison, not knowing it was poison."

Butterworth laughed. "So, the actor and the snake-oil salesman concocted the same plan as the embezzlers. Travel with L. Merryweather Handal, pretend to be wealthy Europeans, get to Mexico and freedom. And spend as much time as possible hunting deer or wild mustangs just in case the law happened by. Besides, I think you city slickers enjoyed this. Too much probably for your own good."

Uneasily, Dave Goldman asked, "So, Butterworth, what's your plan? You're not after the reward."

" 'Course not. The bank's offering ten thousand for Moritz and company, and I'm not sure what the doc and baron will bring but doubt if it's more than five hundred. I'm greedier than that. Nope, my eyes are set on the four hundred thousand Moritz is carrying."

Handal kicked the dirt at his feet. "By Jupiter, do you mean I have been escorting frauds?"

"Yep."

"Including you," Hannah said quietly, eyes trained on the gunman.

She thought Butterworth might turn violent, but he merely nodded.

"You still haven't told us what you did with Buddy and the others," she said.

The dime novelist thundered, "Jumping Jehosophat, my lovely bride was with them. What have you done with Jones, you scoundrel?"

He didn't intimidate Mr. Butterworth at all, but the gunman answered, "She's fine, sir, her honor intact. Can't speak for the one-eyed Texan now, but they were all alive when I left them. 'Course, like y'all, they ain't got no horses. My partner's driving them to join Ramón. You see, I figure we'll leave you folks here, hitch up the wagons full of the Chicago bank money, and mosey on down to Mexico."

"Your partner . . ." Handal began. "That traitor Nehemiah."

That caught the killer off guard. "Who? You mean that squirt?" Butterworth laughed. Handal frowned, his theory destroyed. "No, I mean Carl Klint, or should I say Franco Corrado. All that target practice and our private chats got our embezzler's partner to thinking. He's a turncoat, Moritz, decided he might live longer riding with me than you."

"Not likely," Dave Goldman offered.

Butterworth shrugged. "Yeah," he agreed, "but he don't know that."

Hannah took a step toward the gunman, but stopped when the fake Englishwoman raised the .44 Russian. "What about Buddy?" she asked.

"He took a bullet in the leg. Now, folks, why don't y'all just settle down and relax. As soon as Ramón and Franco come back, we'll hitch up the wagon and leave you folks alone."

But Hannah had one more question. "Turk," she said. "Who killed him?"

"I did." Feeling secure, the gunman shoved the Colt into its holster. "I asked, well, bribed Turk to snoop around, find out whose luggage had that money, or had something that would tell me who I was looking for. Slipped Nehemiah a ten spot, too, but he didn't find nothing. Turk did, but he was a greedy sort. And temperamental, as your beau will attest. Anyway, after that last fight, I come up with a plan. I shot Turk and dumped him in the desert. Only I knew we'd be riding real close to that body. Figured everyone would blame that long-haired mustanger on the deed, and I was right. So that would get him out of my hair—didn't see no need in having to disarm him and Pecos—and increase my share of the booty. But, just to make sure, Little Gene Fintel played his part and made sure Belissari found the body. Then I just happened along."

"So," Tom Rockwall spoke, removing the pipe from his mouth, "you and Lady Guinevere have been in this together all along."

Butterworth shook his head. "Not exactly. Gwen Crooks—you don't mind if I use your real name now, do you?" The witch smiled mirthlessly. "We were both after the same game, only we didn't know it. But we finally realized what we were doing and joined up. Four hundred thousand dollars can go a long way."

Gwen Crooks. A fitting name. Hannah brushed the bangs out of her eyes. Buddy was wounded, Pete in jail, and now she and the others were in the hands of this filthy lot.

"So," Handal said, "you think you have the upper hand on us now, but you don't know me, L. Merryweather Handal. I'll track you down, Butterworth. I'll track you all the way south to the Yukon if need be."

The killer raised his hand. "South? The Yukon?"

"Yes." Handal no longer looked sure of himself.

"It's down south, off the coast of South America. Right?"

"You do your tracking, General," Butterworth said with a grin. "You're welcome to track after me."

At least, Hannah thought, he planned on leaving them alive. Bonaventura spoke as much, "You leave us alive, no?"

"Sure, honey," Butterworth said. "I ain't never shot a woman, don't intend on starting now. And shooting a snake like Turk in the back, or fools on a stagecoach who think they can take me, well that's one thing. But shooting down a bunch of folks lost in this forgotten country is no way to save ammunition. So no one gets hurt here, unless you try something foolish. But after I leave, if you happen to die in the desert, well, it won't be my fault."

"You all right?" Pete asked.

Buddy Pecos grimaced. "No, I ain't all right, you fool. I been shot in the thigh. Shot by a six-year-old, snot-nosed kid. You stupid—" He would have gone on like that, so Belissari tightened the bandana over the bullet wound, causing Buddy to yell, curse, and spit.

He had found them at Novena Spring, all tied except Pecos, who lay bleeding by the water hole. Butterworth had beaten Doc Schnitzler badly—bruises masked the man's face, and his left eye was swollen shut—but Nehemiah and Jones Handal seemed all right, or would be as soon as they got the blood flowing to their hands again.

Pete assumed Butterworth had wounded Pecos. But

the Texan said otherwise, and he didn't sound delirious. "The boy?" Pete was skeptical.

"Yeah, the boy!" Buddy snapped. "Butterworth was beatin' the tarnation out of the doc when I come up on him from behind. He and that young Klint, the others was already tied up, 'cept Eugene. So I drawed my Schofield and told 'em, 'Hands up.' And they obeyed, sure as Sunday. Then that boy pulled a Navy Colt and shot me in the leg."

"Laughed about it, too," Jones Handal chimed in.

The gunman groaned and told Pete through clenched teeth: "So help me, Pete, if Hannah thinks she's gonna adopt that boy after all of this is over with, I'll shoot her and the kid both."

Belissari pushed his hat back. Buddy had lost some blood, but the bone had not been broken, and the bullet went all the way through. He wouldn't be able to fork a horse for a while, or help Pete track down Horace Wilbur Butterworth, but he wasn't likely to die, either.

But . . . Eugene? What was going on?

"Butterworth and the boy rode double back toward base camp. The Klint boy took our livestock, guns as well. Butterworth told him to meet up with Ramón and bring just enough horses for a wagon and some riders. They'd leave the rest at a water hole."

"Outlaw Hole," Pete said.

"Nope. That's where base camp is."

So Butterworth had partners, the *vaquero*, Carl Klint, and Eugene. That meant—Pete's stomach turned—the boy's mother was in on this, also. Belissari smoothed his mustache, thinking. At least,

Butterworth didn't appear to be planning another murder. If that had been the case, everyone here would be dead. No, he would leave Hannah and the others stranded at Outlaw Hole.

"You gonna get that bushwhacker?" Jones asked.

"I plan to," Pete answered.

But how? He'd have to get to Outlaw Hole before Butterworth and the gang pulled out. He checked the sinking sun. Most likely first thing in the morning, the country being too rugged to travel in wagons at night. Pete would need a horse to get to the basin before morning, and lame Penelope couldn't carry him there. The stolen horses, those the outlaws didn't need for themselves, would be near water, most likely Solomon Wooten's old hideout, but that was even farther than base camp.

He sighed, knowing he would never be able to stop Butterworth, not unless he tracked the man down in Mexico, which he wasn't quite ready to rule out. But Hannah, most likely, Goldman, Handal, and the others would be safe. Unless Butterworth decided to take a hostage along just to make sure he reached the south side of the river.

"Why?" he asked aloud. "What is all of this about?"

Dr. Ludwig Schnitzler cleared his throat. "I'm afraid I can explain," he said softly, and told them everything.

With a curse, Jones Handal shook her head and stomped her feet when Nepomuk Barthélemy, alias Dr. Ludwig Schnitzler, finished. "You mean ain't nobody in this group actually plannin' on payin' my honey-dumplins?"

"I fear not," the battered man said. "After I told the truth about me and Barry, Carl . . ." The doctor sighed. "He and Gustave are embezzlers. They stole a tidy sum from a Chicago bank."

"Hey," Nehemiah said, "that's why Mr. Butterworth asked me to look in some luggage if I could. Didn't tell me what I was looking for, just said I'd know when I saw it. Paid me ten dollars even."

"Well," the doctor said. "That explains everything, I guess."

Except how we're getting out of here. Pete grabbed a canteen and walked to the spring. Penelope snorted at him as he squatted and held the canteen under the water. Belissari saw the horse apples nearby and dropped the canteen. He fingered the manure. And when the mare whinnied, Pete thought of another plan.

Chapter Nineteen

The mare's ears pricked forward, and she lifted her head and stared at a ridge several seconds before Pete heard the rumbling of hoofbeats. Gripping the lariat tighter, he peered over the mound of rocks near the water hole where he had hobbled Penelope.

They had pushed the wagon away from the hole, out of sight, and made a cold camp that evening. Pete left Buddy with Nehemiah and the phony doctor and found a decent hiding spot in the rocks. Jones Handal insisted coming with him. They secured the mare, unsaddled, at the edge of the water and waited. Darkness hadn't set in yet, but would soon, and Belissari was about to give up when he heard them.

Mustangs. He had guessed right. A dark stallion topped the ridge and reared, his forelegs pounding the air, while his *manada* of six mares stopped behind him. Seeing Penelope, the stallion galloped down the hill before stopping suddenly about a hundred yards from the water. He whinnied, and the buckskin answered. The other mares slowly drifted down the hill, smelling water, hungering to slake their thirsts, but waiting for the stallion to move first.

"Come on." Belissari only mouthed the words, daring not to speak for even the slightest noise might spook the entire herd. He hoped to lure the animals to the water hole with the mare, spring from his cover, and throw a loop over the neck of the closest animal. He couldn't be particular, although he would prefer the stallion over one of the mares. After that, he'd have to saddlebreak the captured mustang without the luxury of a holding pen. If the horse threw him and Nehemiah and Jones couldn't catch it, they would be exactly where they were before: stranded.

First, though, Pete had to catch a mustang, and he wouldn't be able to do that unless the stallion approached the mare and the water.

The mustang danced along the trail, prancing. Pete held his breath. A white-faced light bay with four short socks, the stallion stood about fifteen hands with powerful legs. He was smart, untrusting. His ears flattened, and he thrust his head up and down, nostrils wrinkled, forelegs pawing the earth, as if he were meeting the challenge of a rival stallion. Suddenly, the bay whirled around and squealed at his *manada*.

"He ain't comin'," Jones Handal whispered.

"Shhhhhhh."

"Shush your ownself."

The Spencer's hammer clicked ominously behind

him. Pete had handed the carbine to Jones before un-saddling Penelope and had forgotten all about it. He turned quickly, saw the leathery, lean woman rise, bring the stock against her right shoulder and fire.

Belissari screamed no.

The mustang squealed.

The mares thundered over the hill and disappeared.

Jones Handal jacked a fresh cartridge into the Spen-cer, shifted the carbine to her left hand, smiled and, pumping her right fist, said triumphantly, "Done it again."

The mustang lay on his side, unmoving. Penelope struggled anxiously against her hobbles, and Pete felt a mixture of bile and vehement curses in the back of this mouth. Blood rushed to his head. His ears burned with fury. But before he could lash out at the woman, Jones pointed a dirty, bony finger at the fallen stallion and said, "Hurry, boy. I just stunned that hoss. Get movin' before he regains his faculties."

Pete moved silently, angrily, crossing the water hole and heading for the downed mustang. Twenty yards from the bay, however, he picked up the pace, jogging first, next sprinting, when he realized the horse wasn't dead. He stood over the stallion, saw the dark eye blink, and quickly he knelt and slipped a loop over the animal's head.

The .50–70 bullet had grazed the spinal nerve just above the withers. A little blood trickled into the bay's mane, and slowly the horse began to kick with his forefeet. Pete gazed, unbelieving. Jones Handal had made a perfect crease shot, hitting a moving target a hundred yards away in fading light with a battered old Tenth Cavalry carbine she had never once fired.

A minute later, the mustang rolled over and scrambled to his feet, shaking his head back and forth, trying to realize what had happened. Belissari braced the lariat against his back and dug his moccasins into the earth, preparing himself for the fight sure to come. But Jones Handal moved in front of him, setting the Spencer on the ground, and gently grabbing the rope between Pete and the mustang.

"Hoh, hoh, hoh, hoh, hoh," she told the horse, shook her head and snorted. Slowly, she worked her way up the rope, grunting, pawing the ground with her right foot, never taking her eyes off the mustang, which stared at her uncertainly. The stallion, however, didn't fight the lariat, didn't even move. "Shuh," she told the bay, and now stood in front of the animal. Jones released her hold on the lariat and patted the horse just above his mouth. She pulled herself closer and sent her hot breath up the mustang's nostrils.

Still, the mustang did not move.

"Petey," Jones said softly. "Fetch me a blanket, will ye?"

Mesmerized, Belissari obeyed. When he returned with the woolen blanket, she took it and tossed it over the mustang's head. She rubbed the stallion's nose, led the animal to the water, and removed the blanket. Once at the hole, Pete removed Penelope's hobbles and herded her toward the wagon, leaving Jones alone with the wounded beast. The mustang drank while she slapped a mud poultice over the bullet wound. By the time Belissari returned, Jones was massaging the stallion's body, working her way over his flanks and down his legs, occasionally mumbling a "shuh" or a "hoh-hoh." The blanket once again covered the horse's eyes. He stood docile.

Finished, she patted the mustang's neck and smiled at Pete.

"You got a lot to learn about mustangs, Petey," she said. "He's got my scent. Trusts me. I told him I was all right, wouldn't hurt him no more, told him you was all right, too. Come over here and breathe into his nose, let him catch your scent."

Pete didn't feel incredulous. He had seen too much. He followed Jones Handal as if she were Professor Moore, instructing the University of Louisville students in Latin. Placing his fingers on the side of the horse's mouth, he lifted the mustang's head slightly and sent his hot breath up the horse's nose. He didn't seem to mind.

"Good," Jones said. "He likes your scent. He knows you now. Talk to him, Petey."

Pete muttered something, moved to the mustang's side and patted his neck. Jones told him to rub his body against the animal's belly, so that's what Belissari did. The mustang wasn't the only one stunned. If Jones Handal had told Pete to pretend he was Lady Godiva, he would have.

"Shuh-shuh-shuh," Jones said as she approached the bay. The horse neighed. Jones smiled.

"Better run fetch your saddle, blanket, and bridle, Petey," she said. "That is if you still got a hankerin' to ride to Outlaw Hole and be the hero my honey-dumplins says you is in his books and such."

"We still have to ride the rough out of him," he reminded her, nodding at the horse.

"Hoh-hoh-hoh," she told the mustang, turned to Pete and shook her head. "He's already broken, silly. They ain't no rough left on this gentle fella. And you call yourself a mustanger."

The mustang quivered when Pete threw the saddle on his back, but Jones neighed once, hoh-hohed twice, and shuhed once. Just like that, the bay settled down. Belissari secured the saddle while Jones spoke to the mustang. He shook his head, half-expecting the wild horse to regain his senses and bolt, especially after Jones removed the blanket covering the horse's eyes. Yet the mustang simply shook his head and snorted. Pete grabbed the bridle, pressed his thumb against the bay's mouth, and slipped in the bit and slid the bridle into place. Too easy.

He looked at the horse's ears, turned back as if the mustang felt sleepy, bored or sick. Maybe he was trying to lull his captors into false security. He would explode at any second.

The hard part would begin when he mounted. Belissari put his left foot in the stirrup, grabbed the horn and pulled himself into the saddle. The mustang backed up a little, then stopped.

Jones Handal tossed Pete the Spencer. Still the horse refused to act up.

Nodding slightly, Jones whickered at the stallion before looking up at Belissari. "We'll be waitin' for you here. Soon as you dispatch them villains, come on back and pick us up. I'll look after your one-eyed pard and them others."

Pete looked on blankly.

"What are you waitin' for, you dumb oaf?" Handal scolded. "Time's a-wastin'."

Shoving the carbine into the scabbard, Pete kicked the mustang's sides. Now the powerful beast exploded, sending Belissari's hat sailing, the horsehair stampede string catching underneath Pete's bandana and saving the hat from being left behind. The bay loped past the wagon, where Buddy, Ludwig, and Nehemiah stared in disbelief. The mustang wasn't fighting the bit, wasn't bucking. No, the stallion raced like a well-trained racehorse. Pete leaned forward and rode with his hands, not needing to encourage the bay by kicking or slapping his back.

The night air cooled Belissari's face. He let the mustang pick his path over the rough terrain, then gave him free rein over the flats, guided only by the stars and quarter moon, heading toward Outlaw Hole as if the mustang knew the destination, as if Jones Handal told him where to go.

Pete never spoke. He simply ducked his head and hugged tighter with his thighs, finding a comfortable rhythm with the strong-legged runner's stride. Belissari thought about pulling in the mustang, slowing him, conserving some strength, but decided against it. He would let the stallion set his own gait.

So on ran the mustang . . . flying like winged Pegasus.

Chapter Twenty

Thick dust rose in the morning air as Ramón Armando hitched a team to the Klints' wagon. The animals seemed uncooperative, and the *vaquero* swore angrily in Spanish, first at the horses, then at Carl Klint for not helping. Butterworth told the embezzler to help, and the man Hannah once thought polite did as he was told.

They were taking only the one wagon, with Klint driving it and, apparently, Lady Grotesque and that brat Eugene riding in the back. Ramón and Butterworth would ride horses, but the Mexican had brought two extra saddle mounts. At first Hannah thought the horses were spares, but they were already saddled and bridled. It took a few minutes for reality to hit her.

Hostages.

One of the horse's was Hannah's dun gelding that had been in the remuda.

As soon as the team was hitched, Carl Klint climbed aboard to driver's box and waited. With a smile, Mr. Butterworth approached the captives huddling in a circle near the coals of an old fire. Calmly, he drew his Colt.

"We'll be taking our leave, folks," he said. "But I'll put Ramón atop a rise with a Sharps rifle. And if anyone tries to follow us afoot, he has orders to shoot to kill."

"What about the other horses?" Goldman asked. "Where'd you leave them?"

Butterworth laughed. "Ramón killed them. I told him to slit their throats once he got them herded away from y'all. No shots. Didn't want to risk 'em."

"You killed horses?" the baron said queasily.

"Didn't want you to go horse hunting and find them, or them come to find the water here."

Goldman shot up. "Without horses, we'll die out here! You—"

The Colt exploded. A bullet whined off a rock near Goldy's feet. When the echoes died down, Butterworth pointed the pistol barrel at the Missourian's head. "Sit down," he said, "and shut up before I shut you up."

Goldman sat down.

Clearing his throat, L. Merryweather Handal pushed his hat up but kept his seat, not wanting the gunman to send a bullet in his direction. "Butterworth," he said, "there is a code out in the West, even among vermin such as yourself. You don't shoot a man in the back and you don't leave women folks to die in the desert, hot and painfully, of starvation, snake bite, or sunstroke. I know you're an outlaw, but I also believe you will follow an honorable code. It's the way of the good bad man."

The killer sighed, waited for the long-winded novelist to finish, and was surprised that Handal *was finished*. "Well," Butterworth said, "in case you have forgotten, I put two slugs in Turk's back. But you're right about one thing. I won't leave a lady to dry up in this desert. That's why I'm taking Hannah and Bonaventura with me."

"What about me?" Dagmar Klint wailed.

"You're no lady," Butterworth answered.

He motioned for Hannah and the servant to rise and pointed his barrel at the extra horses. "Those are pretty slow horses," he said, "so don't try to outrun us. Wouldn't want to shoot two pretty gals in the back."

"What'll you do to them?" Goldy asked.

"Don't worry. Once we're across the border, I'll turn them loose. Just figured the added insurance would help in case we run into Rangers before we hit the Rio Grande. And the rest of you, you have water here and food. With luck, some hunting party will come along and take you back to the comforts of civilization." He tipped his hat with the Colt's barrel.

"So long, folks."

Resisting would be futile, might get Goldy, Handal, and many others hurt, or killed. Hannah pulled herself into the dun's saddle and waited. Ramón mounted his gelding, and Lady Going-to-Jail climbed aboard the wagon beside Klint and Eugene crawled into the back.

The wagon began rolling. Armando followed.

Bonaventura gripped the saddle horn with her tiny hands and tried to pull herself up, but the pinto began following the moving horses, and the Italian servant fell on her backside. Hannah started to dismount, stopped. She saw dust rising in the distance, above the hill.

"Pete," she whispered, although he should be in the Fort Davis jail. But it was him. She knew it. The wind, the gods, whispered his name, and she had learned there was something to that Greek mythology, although she'd never admit it. Stall, she told herself. Give him some more time.

The servant was up, never losing the reins, and stopped the horse. She tried again to mount, but her legs were too short. She had trouble lifting a foot to the stirrup. That idiot Ramón should have lowered the stirrups.

Goldman started to help her, but Butterworth spun around and told him to keep his seat. "Get up!" the gunman yelled at Bonaventura. "We ain't got all day."

The pinto still wanted to follow the wagon. Butterworth seemed to realize this and called out to Klint and Armando to stop.

"Whoa!"

Hannah bit her lower lip and turned away from the dust. She didn't want anyone to notice what she had spotted.

Bonaventura groaned. Butterworth cursed, dropped the reins to his horse and holstered his revolver.

"Here," he said angrily, and reached to help the servant. Only she spun and clawed his cheek, slicing it to bone, kicked him hard in the stomach, and as the pinto bolted from her, she bounded twice and hurled herself into the saddle, screaming at the top of her lungs, riding as if she had been born on horseback.

Slapping his bloodied face with his left hand, Mr. Butterworth, on his knees, drew the Colt and swore. Hannah kicked the dun. Butterworth turned, saw the gelding, and tried to get out of its way. Too late. The horse knocked the gunman over, and Hannah leaped from the saddle. She landed on her feet, somehow maintained her balance, and kicked Mr. Butterworth in the nose. He fell backward, moaned, rolled over, far from finished. The Colt had fallen out of his hand, lay in the dirt a few feet from Hannah. She ran for it, felt Butterworth's harsh grip on her left calf, knew she was falling.

She tasted dirt, blinked, saw the Colt, reached for it. Butterworth pulled her back. Hannah rolled over, kicking at the gunman with her free leg. Her heel caught the gunman's nose again. Blood spurted. He let her go. She turned, caught her breath, dived for the pistol, clutched the barrel, pulled it closer.

Breath exploded from her lungs. She screamed, dropped the Colt, rolled onto her back, reached for her aching ribs where Butterworth's boots had connected. Pain blurred her vision, but she saw the gunman over her, bend, pick up his revolver, cock the hammer.

Next she heard a sickening thud. Hannah's vision cleared in time to see Mr. Butterworth's cold eyes roll back into his head. He dropped the gun. Then he fell sideways, revealing L. Merryweather Handal, iron skillet in hand, breathing heavily.

"Are you all right?" Handal asked.

Hannah nodded too soon. A bullet ricocheted near the ground. Handal dived for cover, dropping his skillet. She spotted Carl Klint on the ground near the buckboard. He levered a Winchester and aimed again. This bullet struck closer. Hannah dived again for Butterworth's Colt, found it, drew it closer even though Klint stood well out of pistol range.

A rifle boomed, then another, the shots reverberating against the rocky walls of Outlaw Hole. But these came from the opposite direction. She turned, saw a rider on a light bay mustang charging toward them, reins in his teeth, his face disappearing briefly in the smoke as he fired his carbine.

Then came another shot. Friendly fire. Dave Goldman had caught up with Butterworth's horse, jerked a Winchester from the scabbard, and sent a volley at the covered wagon.

"Watch Eugene," Hannah found herself saying.

"What for?" L. Merryweather Handal responded. "He shot Pecos, remember?"

Ramón Armando spun around in the saddle, clawing for a weapon. His horse squealed and he toppled from the saddle, rolling over an ocotillo plant and screaming as the cactus spines ripped his flesh. He landed against a yucca, its leaves spearing him, and sat up on his knees, bloody, dirty hands over his head, pleading, "*No mas. No mas. No mas.*"

The rider raced past them. Hannah caught her

breath. It was Pete. He fired again, and Carl Klint grasped his left thigh, rifle clattering against the rocks.

"Don't shoot!" he yelled.

The covered wagon bolted forward, horses struggling to top the rise, kicking up dust. Lady Get-Out-Of-Here screamed at the animals, snapping the heavy reins, cursing, her voice carrying not even a hint of a British accent. The incline was too steep for the wagon. A bedroll toppled out of the back, followed by a crate, followed by a flour barrel, followed by little Eugene. He cried out, hit the ground with a splat, and lay still.

Pete Belissari pitched the empty Spencer, drew the revolver and followed the wagon. It lumbered up the hill, reached the incline, disappeared in more dust. The mustang flew after the wagon, barely laboring as he climbed the hill. Belisarri fired once, knowing he couldn't hit anyone and not wanting to, but wanting, hoping Guinevere would stop.

She couldn't escape. Didn't have a chance.

He heard her shouts as she whipped the team furiously. He thought the team might break the traces and send the wagon out of control, crashing over a hillside, crushing the lovely redhead to death. Again, he gave the mustang free rein, closed in on the wagon. The front wheel hit a rock, and the wagon jumped, skipped and slammed on its side, sending the Englishwoman into the rocks as the horses broke free and sprinted away.

Belissari reined up, leapt from the horse, and raced to Guinevere. Shoving the Remington into his waistband, he gently rolled her over, grimaced at the nasty gash on her forehead. Her eyes fluttered, opened. She smiled.

"It's over," he told her.

"No," she said, and planted a rock against the side of his head.

The blow didn't knock him out, just stunned him. It felt as if he were watching from a distant peak, watching Lady Guinevere, watching himself. He saw her stand over him, pull out the Remington and walk over the loose rocks to the waiting mustang. He saw himself call out for her to stop, saw her laugh, saw her grab the reins and swing into the saddle. He saw the mustang buck angrily and send her flying, somersaulting in midair and landing in a patch of prickly pear. He saw himself snicker, saw himself say, "He don't like your scent."

Chapter Twenty-one

"**O**w!"

"Hold still."

"You try holding still while you're stitching up my head with horsehair."

Hannah lowered the needle threaded with the bay stallion's hair from its tail. She reached over and kissed Pete's forehead.

"Better?" she asked.

He shrugged. She made another stitch.

"Ow!"

Pete was the last patient. Hannah had patched up Mr. Butterworth, Ramón, Carl Klint, Lady Gory, and little Eugene. Dave Goldman and Merryweather Handal tied them up.

After testing Hannah's sewing job, Belissari headed for the mustang.

"Pete," Hannah pleaded.

He waved her off. "Somebody has to track down Bonaventura, tell her everything's all right, bring her back." Pete winked at Goldy. "Dave would appreciate it."

"No need," Tom Rockwall said, and everyone looked at him, first at his smiling eyes over the spade beard, then at the Colt revolver in his massive hand. "She knew what she was doing."

Pete nodded. "I guess if the baron and the doctor are frauds, it stands to reason that their servant is one, too."

The black man smiled. "Mr. Belissari, I am impressed. The University of Louisville must be an excellent school."

"And you?" Hannah asked.

With his left hand, he withdrew a wallet from his inside vest pocket and tossed it toward her. She caught the glint of sunlight against metal as it flapped open and landed near her feet. Hannah stooped, picked it up, opened it, looked back at Rockwall.

"Pinkerton agent?"

"Yes," he said. "I've been on the trail of our bank embezzlers for a while. Tried to make everyone suspicious of everyone else so they wouldn't pay much attention to me. I thought briefly about nabbing the embezzlers at Fort Davis, once I was sure it was them. But then I realized the truth about our good baron and Doc Ludwig. Then our friend Turk got himself killed.

Then I sent off a wire and learned that Mr. Butterworth wasn't a nice sort of fellow. So I decided to see how this hand played out."

Hannah swore angrily. "You, a Pinkerton agent, and you left Pete in jail. What if they had hanged him for a murder he didn't commit?"

Rockwall snickered. "Hang him? Pete? Lady, the only way a jury out here would ever convict Pete of anything was if he burned down a jail or something. He's a likable fella."

"What's your game?" Hannah asked. "The rewards?"

He shook his head. "Not for Pinkerton agents. No, I was thinking about that four hundred thousand dollars."

"Oh." Hannah sighed.

"And Bonaventura?" Goldy asked.

"Don't fret. I saw Butterworth fill his saddlebags with some of that stolen cash. She saw it, too. I figure she's halfway to Mexico by now, maybe even there."

"What's her real name?" Gen. Handal asked.

Rockwall shrugged. "I can't solve all the mysteries, folks."

"So you leave us here, the same as Butterworth planned?" Pete asked.

"No," Rockwall said, "I shoot you all like dogs." He waited, laughed, and shook his head. "Just joshing. Now, if a couple of you would so kindly hitch a team to a wagon and load the Klints' trunk of money, I'll be out of your hair."

They heard the pounding of hooves, saw the rising dust. Rockwall turned as a galloping pinto topped the rise. He lowered his gun, staring incredulously. "What's she doing?" he asked. "Coming back?"

He spun around quickly, snapped off a shot at Goldy, who was running toward Bonaventura, screaming at her to turn back, that Rockwall would kill her. Goldman stopped. The gun rotated to train on Pete's head. Pete sat back down. Rockwall turned, just in time to meet the lowered head of the pinto, ridden expertly by Bonaventura, or whatever her name was.

Tom Rockwall collapsed in a heap.

Hannah Scott stitched him up, too.

The mustang snorted as Pete pulled himself wearily in the saddle. He glanced at the prisoners, wondered how they would ever haul so many back to Fort Davis. That made his stomach turn. He had almost forgotten about the fire, the burned-down jail. Tom Rockwall's comment floated through his mind. *Lady, the only way a jury out here would ever convict Pete of anything was if he burned down a jail or something.*

He looked at Bonaventura and Goldy. That made him feel better. Isabella Fiamma, alias Bonaventura, alias The Roman Flame, alias Raven Child, alias Dark Eyes, could have escaped to Mexico. That had been her plan. She had recognized Lady Guinevere, who had recognized Dagmar Klint, and slowly pieced together this mystery, planning to take a share of the loot and maybe open up a *cantina* in Mexico City. But she couldn't leave Dave Goldman, sweet, kind, good-kissing Goldy, in the desert. So she came back. And saved them all in the process.

"I'll be back with the horses," Pete told Hannah.

"Butterworth said Ramón killed them," Handal interjected.

"Butterworth told Ramón to kill them," Pete corrected. "But you remember Ramón. He couldn't kill that dying deer. He's not one to kill horses. And Carl Klint didn't have the guts to do it." Glancing at the bound men, he asked, "Right, fellows?"

"*Sí*," the *vaquero* answered sheepishly.

"All right," Pete said, gathering the reins. "I'll be back with the horses this evening. Then we'll swing up to get Buddy and the others, and take our merry troupe to Fort Davis . . . um, no, we'll go to Presidio. Yes, Presidio. We'll take them to Presidio and turn them over to the Rangers."

L. Merryweather Handal clapped his hands. "By jingo, Peter, you've done it again. And that reward money will make up for my expenses. I might even have enough to pay you, Hannah and the rest."

Belissari cleared his throat. "Actually, General," he said, "I'm thinking that money would be better served building a new sheriff's office and jail in Fort Davis."

"What?" Hannah asked.

Pete forced a smile before kicking the mustang into a gallop. He had horses to gather, a lot of work to do. He would have to explain to Hannah about the jail-house fire and everything else . . . but that could wait.

5TH AVE. 12/01